Murder By Plane

T.E.Avery

This is a work of fiction. All of the characters, organizations and events portrayed in this novel are products of the author's imagination or are used fictitiously.

Copywrite 2012 by T.E.Avery. No part of this book may be used without permission of the author.

For Peggy

Chapter 1.

Sunlight glared on the yellow cab as it rolled to a stop on the driveway of a house overlooking the Pacific Ocean. A slender girl stepped out of the hot car. She paid the driver with a trembling hand; hesitating a moment before approaching the front door.

The man who killed my sister lives here.

Within the house, Reginald St. John awoke suddenly from a nightmare. Soaked in sweat, he sat up in his luxurious bed, having dreamed about killing Germans and a plane crash. His heart was beating rapidly. He felt disoriented and queasy, the room was spinning and his ears were pounding.

Reginald opened his eyes and looked around, uncertain of the time or his whereabouts.

"Too much to drink," he muttered as he tried to extract himself from a tangle of twisted silk sheets.

His mouth tasted as dry as a dusty road and his eyes felt like someone had sprinkled sand into them. The pounding continued and he realized it was coming from the bedroom door.

"Stop that noise," he yelled at the door and then held his hands over his throbbing head. Bits and pieces of the dream floated like cobwebs through his brain, the same nightmare that had plagued him since the accident almost a year ago. A wave of grief washed over him, as always, when he thought of the plane crash and Lillian.

"Don't think about it," he told himself. "I need a drink. Where is that bottle?"

The door to his bedroom burst open and his driver, Dominic, filled the doorway.

"You okay boss? I hear you make the noise again; the scream. I knock, but you don't answer."

"Yes. Yes. I'm all right. You know I have that same dream from time to time since the accident last year. Have you seen the whisky I was sipping last night?"

"You sip it all." The big Sicilian spread his arms.

"I don't remember drinking the entire bottle."

2. T.E.Avery

Dominic just raised his hands with palms up. "I don't know where it is boss. Okay? You don't need that stuff. You need something to eat. Why don't you go downstairs and Greta fix you up with a nice breakfast now?"

"What day is it Dominic?"

"It Monday. You go eat now. You feel better."

"What time is it?"

"After four. You eat." The big man turned and walked out shaking his head and talking quietly to himself in Sicilian. Suddenly he stopped and turned. "I forget. Miss Moxley. She downstairs waitin to see you."

Reginald's legs were still wrapped in the sheets and he almost fell out of bed as he struggled to rise. Drinking all night and sleeping away the days had been his routine for most of the year, 1934. "Alexis Moxley?"

"Yeah boss, Miss Moxley."

"Good lord, what does she want?"

"I don't know. She just show up not too long ago. She waitin in the foyer."

"Oh, all right then. Keep her waiting for a while longer. I'll be right down. Good grief."

Reginald stumbled into the bathroom, slumping forward, staring at his reflection in the mirror. Strands of dark lanky hair fell across his bloodshot eyes, betraying last night's alcoholic binge. "You could hardly be one of the most successful stars in Hollywood," he told the image. Reginald rubbed a hand over the stubble on his chin and squinted. His once stylish pencil mustache now appeared shabby, hiding the scar that ran from the side of his upper lip. Reginald thought he looked older than his actual thirty-nine years.

"You sir, are disgusting," he muttered at his likeness while splashing water on his face.

Murder By Plane 3.

Reginald's thoughts returned to the great war and all of the dreams and the memories buried deeply in his subconscious. He pondered whether these memories were the cause of his recent gloominess or if it could be the devastating plane crash last year which claimed his fiancée's life.

Reginald finally made his way downstairs to his outdoor breakfast table, carefully avoiding the front foyer, dressed in pajama bottoms, robe and slippers. Even under the shade of a large awning, the air felt boiling, a breeze from the ocean provided some small relief. A light breakfast of pastries and fruit, set before him by Greta, his Austrian cook, awaited him. Because of the heat, he had requested strong iced tea instead of his usual coffee.

"Thank you Greta, everything looks wonderful," he said without enthusiasm.

"Will there be anything else Mr. St. John?"

"Yes. Is Miss Moxley still here?"

"She is waiting in the front entry sir," the cook replied tersely.

"Well, I suppose I will have to see her sooner or later. Show her out here Greta."

"Yes sir."

A newspaper lay neatly folded near his plate. The shaded table was situated on a small stone patio surrounded on three sides by a low stucco wall that matched the house. A neat palm lined lawn led down to the beach. The Pacific Ocean spread out unobstructed before him.

The wind from the sea brought with it a pleasant mixture of brine and flowers from the garden. Despite the heat, it was a beautiful day to be outside, but Reginald had as much difficulty enjoying the day as he had falling asleep at night. He blamed himself for the accident that had ended the life of the only woman he had ever loved. The only remedy seemed to be losing himself in alcohol every day. This was how he kept the dreadful memories at bay. He took a small sip of tea and looked out at the endless expanse of water. He wondered what it would be like to swim out there and never come back, to be free from all worries and the constant nagging guilt.

His mind came back to the present as sudden movement drew his attention toward the patio door. Reginald squinted in the bright afternoon light reflecting in the glass as his eyes widened in surprise. His heartbeat increased dramatically as he thought for a moment that he was looking at his dead fiancée.

"God Reggie, you look like death." Alexis Moxley said, in her young and sometimes irritating voice, as she opened the door. Lillian's younger sister, who had recently arrived in Hollywood, was the last person Reginald wanted to see.

"Oh, its you. I momentarily forgot you were waiting," he said.

"Sorry toots. I didn't mean to startle you. You look as if you've seen a ghost." She realized why he had looked so shocked. Although Alexis was slightly shorter, she could still pass as a twin to her dead sister.

"Oh, I really am sorry Reggie." Her eyes brimmed with tears. She sat down without being asked and took his hand in both of hers.

"What are you talking about Alexis?" Reginald asked curtly.

"Oh nothing," she dropped his hand and turned to look at the Pacific. The ocean breeze stirred her shoulder length, strawberry blond, curls under a stylish feathered hat. "I just love this place. It's so nice and peaceful here."

Reginald watched as she helped herself to a large jelly-filled Danish. She continued to small-talk as she ate the roll. "You don't seem to be very hungry and you're still not dressed. Rough night?"

"You could say that." He stared at her perfect features and crumb covered full lips.

"You Kansas girls really do have hearty appetites though."

"I'm not from Kansas and you know it," she said with obvious exasperation. "I haven't eaten all day and I'm starved."

"Apart from your appetite, what brings you to Cirrhosis by the Sea, Alexis?"

He knew that his feelings of irritation toward her were probably based on the guilt he felt over the death of her sister. A younger version of Lillian only increased his unease.

She didn't notice his discomfort and, in fact, appeared to be quite relaxed. After finishing most of Reginald's breakfast, Alexis leaned back and propped her sandaled feet onto the arm of his chair, causing her dress to slide above her knees. Reginald couldn't help staring at her shapely legs. Just as quickly, she dropped her feet to the ground and leaned forward. "Reggie, you haven't worked in a year and your public is beginning to forget you. You've got to pull yourself together and find a way to heal your emotional wounds. You need to get on with your life. I came here to let you know I never blamed you for Lillian's death."

Reginald dropped his eyes at the mention of the accident. He cleared his throat and in a near whisper said, "But I do." Then louder. "So, did you come here to analyze me?"

"No, I came here to tell you something about the accident that I've just recently discovered," the young woman said.

"Alexis please, will you just leave it alone? Nothing that you can say or do will bring Lillian back."

"I know I can't bring Lillie back Reggie." She was back on her feet now and pacing the small enclosure. "Will you just sit there and listen to me for a few minutes and then you can decide for yourself if what I have to say is important?"

"I suppose I could if you would slow down," he said

with a sarcastic smirk. "You said that you have some new information?"

"Yes. You know that I've been working at the Fairmont Studios since I moved here. I managed to get a secretary position with the personnel department. I'm just one of several girls who work there. It's not much, but it pays the rent while I try to get my acting career going."

"Why don't you just tell them that you are Lillian's sister? I'm sure that would open a few doors."

"Oh no, Reggie. I couldn't capitalize on my dead sister. It just wouldn't be right. Anyway, I have a friend from the secretary pool. Her name is Molly and I just met her by chance one day. She helped me get the job."

"How convenient for you, but what about the new information?" he asked.

"I'm getting to that. Molly's boyfriend is a policeman who was at the accident scene a year ago." Alexis paced the small patio as she excitedly related her news. Reginald tried his best to keep up, but finally crossed his arms and slumped lower in the chair.

"This cop told her that the accident had originally been entered on the report as possible sabotage."
Alexis stopped her frantic back and forth movement and arm waving when she loudly pronounced the final word.

Reginald stared back with half closed eyes. "So?"

"Is that all you can say?" She stamped her foot in frustration and wilted into a chair.

"I thought I had found out something big here."

"What good does it do to find out it may have been deliberately planned? It doesn't matter what made the wheel fall off. I still should have brought us down safely. I experienced much worse landings in the war and as a stunt pilot. I should have been able to land that Nieuport." Reginald leaned forward, his head in his hands and then ran his fingers through his hair.

"So you've been blaming yourself because you thought your piloting skills were in question?"

Murder By Plane 7.

"I suppose I have," he said with resignation.

"Look Reggie. I have a suggestion to make."

He slowly sat up and met her emerald gaze. "What is it?"

"Well, I didn't move to California just to become an actress. Oh, don't get me wrong, I want to become a star one day, but I have another motive. I came here to find out what really happened to my sister. That's why I got the job at the studio. When I came here for the funeral, I just had a strange feeling something wasn't quite right about the cause of the accident. I've had almost a year to mull it over while I was finishing college and it still just doesn't add up. I'm not a pilot or a mechanic, but even I know that airplane wheels don't just fall off by themselves."

A lingering pause hung in the air.

"What are you thinking Reggie?"

"I am thinking that you may have a point. Those wheels are quite secure and usually do not detach themselves. I know my mechanic, Don Denison, was thoroughly questioned by the police and the Department of Transportation. Don said the aircraft undercarriage had recently been checked and all had seemed to be in order. He also said there was a cotter pin holding a castle nut in place, if I recall correctly. The pin would have to be removed in order for the castle nut to slowly work itself off of the axle. This would lead to the wheel falling off."

"Didn't you have a lot of experience with that type of airplane during the war? How many times do you remember the wheels falling off of those biplanes Reggie?"

"I do not recall any instances of a Nieuport 12 losing its wheels unless it was during a crash or from enemy fire. Those planes were solidly built."

"So you think that it is possible someone deliberately tampered with your plane and caused the wheel to come off?" she asked.

8. T.E.Avery

"All this time I have been trying to forget what happened. I have never thought about why the wheel would have come off on takeoff."

"Did you actually see it fall off of the plane?"

"No, but there were witnesses on the ground who saw it fall shortly after we were in the air. They had no way of communicating to me that I had lost a wheel. If I had known I could have compensated during landing and set down without any trouble."

"But you didn't know and it wasn't your fault," she said. Can you see that now?"

"I know you are trying to help, but I still feel responsible for that crash," Reginald said.

"Okay, stop with the self-incrimination Reggie," she said. "We need to start thinking about this logically. Now, do you think it was just an accident or could it have been intentional?"

Reginald leaned back and turned to stare at the sea. "I don't know. I suppose it could have been sabotage. But who would do such a thing and why?"

Out of the corner of her eye, Alexis noticed a quick movement of shadows on the trunk of a palm, close to the wall of the house. There was something about the sudden appearance of the form that attracted her attention. She motioned to Reginald and pointed in the direction of the mysterious shade. As soon as he turned to look, the shadow disappeared.

"Did you see that?" Alexis asked.

"See what?"

"That shadow on the palm tree. It looked like there could have been a person hiding behind the wall," Alexis said as she moved to the corner and peered around.

"It was probably Pedro trimming the shrubs along the side of the house," Reginald stated.

"Yeah, or it could have been someone listening in on our conversation. Where is that chauffeur of yours, by the way?" she asked.

Murder By Plane 9.

"Dominic? He had some errands to run. Why do you ask?"

"Have you known him very long?" she asked. "He seems sinister."

"I have known him for a long time and I trust him completely," Reginald said.

The cook came out with a tray containing two glasses of fresh iced tea with lemon.

"Is there a place where we could talk more privately?" Alexis asked.

"You are beginning to sound paranoid." He sipped the tea and made a grimace.

"What's wrong, not alcoholic enough for you?"

"Perhaps if we go inside and I hear you out, you will leave soon," he said.

"And you can start getting plastered again and forget that I was ever here?"

"Yes, that sounds about right. Shall we go inside now? I will have Greta transfer our tea to the study." Reginald rose from his chair.

Alexis grabbed a tall tea glass and walked through the patio doors. Reginald shrugged, reached for his own icy drink, and followed. The interior of the house felt cool and comfortable. A radio broadcast could be faintly heard from another room. The newscaster was talking about the record heat in Los Angeles. Bamboo blinds made the light rake across the room like a shadowy skeleton. Ceiling fans turned slowly in the dark, and expensive Persian carpets were spread across the teak flooring. Framed maps, pictures of sailing ships and a large aquarium covered most of the stucco walls. The effect was that of an exotic bungalow tucked away in some far corner of the world. Alexis looked around with interest, trying to remember the last time she had been here.

This was exactly the kind of place one would expect a man like Reginald St. John to live, she thought. He was someone who had been in the public eye for years, but who still possessed a certain mystery. There was something different about this man who had almost been her brother-in-law. Alexis made a mental note: she would need to find out more about him. Of course it would all depend on her performance in the next few minutes. Reginald opened a slatted door that reminded her of something on a boat. He closed the door after cordially letting her enter first, but his mood changed once they entered the room.

"Now, you have exactly five minutes to tell me what is on your mind." He crossed his arms after flopping down into one of the leather pub chairs that occupied a space on either side of a large window. This opened a breathtaking view of the ocean. A brass telescope on a tripod stood before the window. There were several framed photos above an antique rolltop desk.

She studied the pictures carefully. They were from his years as a flyer in the movies and as a barnstormer. One photo was obviously taken during the war.

A younger Reginald and another squadron mate squatted together in the foreground. The young Reginald appeared serious, but his friend displayed a toothy grin. Two biplanes sat in the background.

"This is a fascinating room," Alexis stated.

"Thank you. It holds many memories. Reginald said. Now back to what we were talking about. The accident and your new theory."

"Yeah, I don't think it was an accident Reggie," she sat in the remaining chair and continued. "That means that Lillian's killer is still running around somewhere."

"Now just a minute Alexis. We don't know that it was intentional. You said the police report originally stated "possible sabotage." That is a long way from proving any real murder."

"Yes, but what if it's true? Wouldn't you want to find the person responsible?" she asked.

"Of course I would, if it were really true," he said.

Murder By Plane 11.

"So you will help me Reggie?"

"Now I did not say that Alexis. I only answered your question," Reginald said.

"But we need to find out if it really was an accident or something … else. Can you just agree to use your influence to find out now what you should have found out last year?"

Her remark had the same effect as a slap and he turned his head away as if it had been struck.

"All right. I will do what I can. Please leave," he said crisply to mask his emotions.

Chapter 2.

She grasped his hand tightly; a single tear ran down her cheek. Reginald looked down at her hand as she self-consciously withdrew it to wipe the tears from her eyes. They sat in awkward silence for several seconds before she sniffed and spoke.

"So, where do we start?"

Reginald rubbed his eyes and shook his head slightly.

"I don't really know where to begin. I have never investigated an aircraft accident and it has been nearly a year."

"I don't believe it was an accident Reggie. I know that it won't bring Lillie back, but I have to find the truth."

Until now, he had not looked at her face, but at the mention of his dead fiancée, Reginald met her eyes and saw a fierce determination.

"I want to know what really happened too," he said.

Alexis crossed her legs. "I've been asking a lot of questions around the studio the last couple of weeks. My plan has been to find someone who may have witnessed something or who knows someone who did. Do you think I should continue?"

"Yes, it can't hurt to make more inquiries. How has the management been treating you?"

The leather chair squeaked as she leaned back.

"I don't know Reggie, I've gotten some strange looks and I've even been reprimanded for spending too much time on personal business. The supervisor is an old bag with a surly attitude who told me to get back to work or start looking for another job."

"I think we could find out more if it were you asking around," she continued.

"I don't know about that Alexis. I have not been on the best of terms with the studio lately." He quickly held his hand up as she started to bristle, and then continued.

"But of course, I will do whatever I possibly can to ferret out more information about the crash. You just keep probing about at the studio. Something is bound to arise eventually. I will talk to the police officer who was on the scene of the accident and to the aircraft mechanic. I know the studio security people will have nothing to say to us."

She studied his handsome, somewhat scruffy, face as he spoke. He looked so drained that it was difficult to imagine him mustering the energy even to dress, much less start an investigation, but what choice did she have?

"What else have you learned from your co-workers besides the earth shattering news about possible sabotage?" he asked.

She ignored the sarcasm.

"Well, I did find out that Bruno Von Heller, the producer, director, studio mogul was romantically interested in Lillie from the time she first set foot in Hollywood."

Reginald's look told her he already knew this.

"Yes, Bruno Von Heller and I go way back. I worked for him for several years before I became successful. I also knew he was interested in Lillian, but she was not interested in him. She once compared him to an evil, fat spider," he chuckled.

Alexis smiled. It was the first time she had seen him laugh, except in the movies.

"How serious do you think Von Heller was about Lillie? I mean, do you think he was in love with her?"

"No, I do not believe Bruno is capable of love. He most likely wanted her as a trophy."

"What happened?" Alexis asked.

"I happened, I think. We met on the set of our first picture together. Lillian was only in a supporting role, but her acting was so outstanding that she soon became the center of attention, much to the chagrin of the lead actress. Lillian was so beautiful and talented. We became friends and then ... more."

"What was Von Heller's reaction when he found out about you and Lillie?" she asked.

"We have not spoken to each other since, at least not

14. T.E.Avery

on a personal level. I think Bruno must have been furious at her for rejecting his advances and at me for 'getting the girl', as they say."

"Do you think he's the type that could do something to hurt someone?"

"I have no doubt that he could and has caused harm to people. I am certain the man has no conscience."

"Von Heller could have sabotaged your airplane Reggie." she stated.

"Technically it was his plane. He owns part of the studio and everything in it. Surely he would not have caused an accident at his own studio?"

"Why not? You just said he is capable of anything. Why not murder?"

"Think of the bad publicity it would cause if he were found out. It would ruin him."

"He may have been motivated by jealousy and spite. Evil, fat spider, remember?"

She wiggled her fingers close to his face simulating the motion of a creepy creature.

"You really can be so annoying," he said flatly.

Alexis ignored his remark. "Hey, I just thought of something else Reggie," What were you saying earlier about the actress who was the lead when you first met Lillie?"

Reginald's puzzled frown indicated his confusion.

"What are you talking about? I am not following you?"

Alexis frowned and kicked his shin.

"You know. The star that was in the movie with you and Lillie," she said.

"Ouch. Calm down. I am trying to think. Oh, you mean Claire Cauldwell. She was my costar in the beginning," he said.

"What do you mean?" Alexis asked.

"About what?" he yawned.

She kicked his lower leg again. "You said, "in the beginning." What do you mean?"

Murder By Plane 15.

"Look here girl. You must control yourself and stop kicking me. Claire was a silent movie star who had the looks, but not the voice. She just never made the transition over to talkies. Claire had a thick Brooklyn accent and was prone to staring at the sound boom. Poor girl, some stage training would have helped."

"What happened on that set Reggie?"

"Claire had a breakdown during filming. She left the set. They asked Lillian to take over the starring role. Your sister was a true performer, made for the part or the part for her. In that one moment a film career ended and another began."

"What ever became of Claire Cauldwell?" Alexis asked.

"I don't know. She was never seen at the studio again."

"Could she have been motivated by revenge?"

"Are you trying to suggest, that Claire Cauldwell could have been the one who rigged the plane to crash? That would certainly be a stretch."

"Well, it was just a thought," Alexis extended her lower lip.

"That is not a very convincing pout. You must practice a little more and don't even think about kicking me again," he pointed.

Just then, they both heard a slight scuffing on the carpeted floor in the outer room and a shadow moved under the door. Reginald stepped across the small space and flung the door wide, only to find the Austrian cook standing, just outside, with a startled look on her face.

"Greta, what are you doing?"

"I ah ... I thought it is time for your afternoon brandy sir," the woman said with surprise.

"Oh yes, it is past time." He all but rubbed his hands in anticipation. "Will you join me Alexis?"

"No thanks. I have to be on my way. Reggie, have you given serious consideration to what we have discussed?"

16. T.E.Avery

"Of course I have, but let us not get too carried away with speculation. Look, I have an old friend who also happens to be my lawyer. He is in that picture on the wall that you were looking at earlier. I am sure he must employ a private investigator and may be able to help clear this up. I will call him tonight and get things started."

"He was in the war?"

"Yes, and he flew after the war too, until he injured his leg in a smashup. He studied law after that and has been my legal representative for many years. His name is Clyde Carver, but we called him Max."

"Okay Reggie, but I'm still going to do whatever I can to find the truth. I've only been in Hollywood for a few months though and I need your help."

"That is why I am going to hire a professional detective to look into this for us. He will bring to light information that we would never be able to find out." The cook came in with the brandy and they both stopped talking. "How are you getting home? Do you have a car or did you travel by cab?"

"I came here in a cab and was going to call another to get home," Alexis said.

"My driver should have returned by now and can give you a ride into town."

"I would appreciate it very much." It occurred to her that he was suddenly behaving much nicer than he had earlier.

"Right. I will finish my drink and escort you to the garage to locate Dominic," he said.

"Reggie, how long have you known that cook of yours?" she asked as they crossed the open space between the house and garage. "It seemed as though she was listening at the door."

"She has only been in my employment for about three weeks. My regular cook, Grace, was injured in an automobile accident and I needed someone to temporarily replace her.

I am unable to prepare anything edible and I do not dine out often."

"How badly was she injured?"

"Her leg was broken and the doctor said it will be several more weeks before she is able to return to work. Are you trying to insinuate that my housekeeping staff is less than trustworthy?"

"Well, maybe."

Reginald and Alexis entered the garage through a side door and observed the Duesenberg was indeed inside. Dominic was just clanging the hood shut as they approached the front of the car. The garage had a small workshop with tools hanging on one wall above a well-used wooden bench.

"Tuning up the old girl, Dominic?"

"Yeah boss. She needed some new spark plugs."

"I would like you to drive Miss Moxley home please."

"Okay boss."

Alexis felt a surge of excitement as Dominic opened the shiny door and Reginald handed her into the spacious backseat.

"Thank you Reggie," she said breathlessly.

"I'll see you later Kansas."

Her smile faded.

"Reginald, don't forget what we talked about," she said sternly.

"I will not forget." He bent down, touched her chin and unexpectedly pecked her on the cheek.

Later, back in his study, drinking a second brandy, Reginald began to review all that he and Alexis had discussed. As he thought about the girl, his heart became somewhat lighter. How could he feel attraction for someone who agitated him so? Yet, he had to admit, she was a beautiful young woman.

If she possessed even half of her sister's talent, she could go far. However, why had she not used Lillian's fame to launch her own career?

18. T.E.Avery

She wanted to get into the studio incognito in order to find out what had occurred on that airfield last year, he thought.

"Crazy kid. What does she think she is up to?" he asked aloud.

Reginald still doubted the young woman's theory about the plane accident, but having his lawyer hire a private detective sounded easy enough. He knew if he went to the studio in person, everyone, including the newspapers hounds, would make it a media circus.

"Not much chance to find out anything that way."
He decided to call his lawyer tonight, before he began his ritual of alcoholic inebriation, which he knew would, no doubt, occur soon. What would his life be like, he thought, if he knew he was not the cause of Lillian's death?

"That is a big "If"," Reginald muttered.
His emotions flirted with the idea of redemption as he turned off the phonograph and the old Billy Murray pre-war tune, a song from happier times. Reginald poured another glass of brandy and picked up the telephone.

Two days later, Reginald's housekeeper, Maria, called from his bedroom doorway to inform him that a private detective waited outside.

"Okay Maria. Thanks, I will be down shortly. Have him wait in the living room por favor."

"Si, Mr. St. John."
Ten minutes later, private detective Frank Brogan introduced himself to the shabby looking movie star.

"I am pleased that you could take the time to come out here to speak with me Mr. Brogan. I have just a few questions concerning an accident that occurred nearly a year ago. I want to find out if there is the possibility foul play may have been involved. May I offer you a drink?"

"Sure, I don't mind a drink in the afternoon, Mr. St. John."

Murder By Plane 19.

Reginald poured two glasses of scotch, over ice, and handed one to the private eye.

"Thanks Mr. St. John. This really hits the spot. It's been so hot lately."

Brogan was a big Irish-American, roughly sixty years of age, and he looked like a retired cop with a face that had been used as a punching bag too often.

"What exactly did you have in mind sir?" Brogan asked.

"I want you to ask some questions around the studio and see what you can find out. Surely, there must be someone who remembers the crash that still works at the studio. I also want you to find out anything that you can from the police. I assume that you have contacts with the local police in some form or other?"

"Ah, yes sir. I was on the force a few years ago. I might be able to find out a thing or two."

"I need you to act as my eyes, ears and mouth, Mr. Brogan, as you know it would be quite impossible for me to go about asking questions. Moreover, you must keep this quiet. I do not need the press finding out that I am looking into the accident. Do you understand sir?"

"Yes, Mr. St. John. You want to know if somebody had it out for you or your girlfriend."

"I suppose that is one way to put it Mr. Brogan," Reginald replied curtly.

"But that trail is gonna be pretty cold after a year sir," Brogan said.

"Yes, but there must be someone who knows what really happened. I want answers and if you can't find them I will hire someone who can."

"Yessir Mr. St. John. I'll look around for a couple a-days, ask some questions, real discrete like and then get back to you. Here's my card if you need to talk to me before I call you," Brogan pulled a tattered piece of paper from his dirty wallet, handed it to Reginald and reached out to shake hands.

20. T.E.Avery

"Your lawyer, Mr. Carver, told me to be sure to send his regards to you sir," Brogan continued.

"Thank you Mr. Brogan, I think you have all the instructions you will need to get started, but please call me as soon as you find out anything significant."

"I will sir. Oh, I almost forgot something. Can I have your autograph for my girlfriend?"

As Frank Brogan drove away from the beach villa, he felt pleased with himself and the day's events. He'd got into a nice little gig that would probably pay off bigger than any job he'd ever had. He would just go around town asking a few questions and poking about. "No big deal," he told himself. These Hollywood types were all the same and he knew he could milk this cash cow for a small bundle, if he played his cards right.

That Scotch whisky was top shelf. Not like the cheap hooch he usually drank every day. He had also gotten the autograph for his girl and he knew she would be glad. She was always yaking about movie stars all the time. He also knew she would show him her gratitude in more ways than one and that made him smile. Yes, this day had turned out better than he could have planned. As these pleasant thoughts passed through his simple mind, Frank Brogan didn't have a clue he was being followed.

Reginald tried to reassure himself everything would go smoothly now that he had hired a professional, but somehow it just didn't feel right. For one thing, he wasn't impressed with this Brogan character in the least. The fellow was a crackpot and looked rather sleazy to Reginald. What could Max Carver have been thinking? Why had he sent this sloppy excuse of an ex-copper to help him with his investigation? Maybe his old friend knew more about the private investigator's credentials and Brogan possessed hidden talents of some sort. Reginald had known men like this during the war.

Murder By Plane 21.

Outwardly, they seemed to be bumbling fools, but during the heat of battle, they could always be counted on. Perhaps his first impression of Brogan wasn't very accurate. After all, what do actors know about private investigators? Max had good judgment most of the time. But not always. His lack of good judgment nearly got him killed in a plane crash. Reginald knew he must make a good effort to investigate his own accident or Alexis would make his life a living hell. The girl was spirited and more than a little vexing, he thought. He decided to give Brogan a few days to see what could be turned up and if things didn't start moving along he would call Max.

His thoughts turned to Alexis again as he poured another glass of his special brand of single malt Scotch whisky.

Alexis nibbled the eraser of her yellow, number two, pencil and covertly observed the activity near the door of the storeroom marked "private". The drama began when none other than Bruno Von Heller had entered the personnel offices several minutes ago and motioned for Doris Hawks, the Department Manager, over to the small file room. Doris had nervously complied. The door had been left ajar and the two could be seen pouring over files. Alexis thought Von Heller seemed more agitated than normal.

"Something is up," Alexis murmured. She quickly put her head down and appeared to be hard at work as Von Heller stormed past her small desk and out of the department. The entire office breathed a collective sigh of relief when he had gone.

"What a creep," Alexis said.

"You can say that again," the girl sitting nearest to her said.

"I wonder what is in that private file room?" Alexis asked.

"All kinda trash on people in there," the girl said.

22. T.E.Avery

A plan began to form in Alexis's mind. She thought about what had occurred in the office a few short minutes ago.

"What sort of trash and on who? "

"Who do ya think? They don't care about low-lifes like us. They got to keep stuff about the studio actors so they can keep-em in line, ya know." She loudly popped her gum and continued. "Anytime a star goes someplace they put a tail on-em."

"But how could you know that for sure?"

"I got ways of knowin Sweety. I been here a few years and I seen a thing or two."

"This place really clears out at lunch time."

"Oh yeah, ya got to get away from this nut house or you go crazy. Where you gonna eat?"

"Well, I thought I might meet someone for lunch today," Alexis lied.

She noticed that Doris, rattled by the visit from Von Heller no doubt, had left the file room door ajar.

Alexis waited until everyone exited the department before making her move. With one final look around, she quickly slipped into the small room, an oversized closet with several rows of metal file cabinets dimly lit by one bare overhead light. She checked the first cabinet. Unlocked. Old Mrs. Hawk had been so upset she must have forgot to lock up before lunch, she thought. Alexis slid the drawers open one by one, carefully scanning the papers within. She couldn't believe what she read. Page after page of hand written and typed personal details, newspaper clippings and even photos. The rumors about Von Heller where true. These files contained all sorts of detailed personal information about every actor who worked at the studio, she realized.

No wonder the only one allowed into the storeroom was the manager.

"That old battleaxe," Alexis muttered.

"Now to find Lillian's file." At least they did put them in alphabetical order, she thought with a smile.

Alexis had just opened Lillian's file when the office manager appeared at the door.

"Oh, hello Mrs. Hawks," Alexis grinned nervously.

"What are you doing in here? This room is private."

"I know, but the door …."

"I realized that I had left it open by mistake and returned to lock it. And what do I find?"

"Ah … me," Alexis said sheepishly.

"Gather your things and remove yourself from the studio, at once, young lady."

Chapter 3.

Alexis felt like a complete failure as she sat on the bench with her hand covering her forehead. What was she going to do without a job? In a big, strange, town and she didn't know many people here. She had no way to keep paying for the room she rented or her other expenses.

She thought about her situation and it didn't look very bright. If she couldn't find another job soon, her only option would be to go back home. But what was back home? She had no living relatives and few friends. It seemed to Alexis that her sister had always been the favored one in the family, the one who was destined to be the great movie star, while Alexis was the girl least likely to succeed. Lillian, the golden girl who never did anything wrong and Alexis the clumsy tomboy who never got anything right.

"Now I feel even worse for thinking badly of my poor, dead, sister," she muttered through her tears.

A man wearing a grey fedora and smoking a cigar gave her a curious glance as he walked by. She ignored the unwanted attention.

Alexis had loved and idolized her older sister and she wanted to stay in Hollywood to find out what had really happened to Lillian. But what about her other reasons, she thought? She had also moved to Los Angeles, after graduating from college, in order to find a way to get into the movies.

The unusual site of a beautiful girl sitting alone at lunchtime was beginning to attract the interest of several more passersby. Alexis felt self-conscious, as if there was a big sign around her neck with the word "Fired" written on it. She tried to hold back the tears as her chin began to tremble. She decided to get as far away from the studio as possible.

Alexis had gotten up from the bench when she heard a familiar voice calling out to her from the street. Alexis turned around and to her surprise she saw a big elegant car parked at the curb, Reginald sitting behind the wheel.

Murder By Plane 25.
He was actually shaved and well dressed in a blue double-breasted jacket and smiling like a Cheshire cat.
"Hello Kansas. Do you need a ride?" he asked as he tipped his hat.
She covered her face with both hands as her self-control crumbled. Reginald could see her obvious distress as her shoulders began to shake and he was quickly out of the car and at her side. A small crowd began to gather.
"Let's get out of here Alexis. We can talk in the car." As he turned the big car onto the street, Alexis managed, in a shaky voice, to relate all the unfortunate events that had occurred.
"I feel so dumb Reggie. Why didn't I wait for a better time to go snooping around?"
Reginald drove to a small roadside diner, not far from his home that he had frequented often.
"Let's have some lunch and discuss everything," he said.
"I'm not hungry, but thanks anyway." She put her hand to her head.
"You may feel better after you eat something."
"I'd rather have a stiff drink," she pouted.
"Now you sound like me. Come on, they have the best roast beef sandwich here."
Alexis grudgingly allowed him to take hold of her arm and escort her inside. It was a tiny place with a counter, some tables and window booths. A radio blared out Cole Porter's 'Anything Goes'. The owner, a small Italian man, came rushing over, wiping his hands on a dirty dish towel.
"Mr. St. John. It's been so long since you came in. Have a seat in your favorite corner booth over there. It's so good to see you again."
They ducked into the seat as a nervous waitress came over to take their orders.
Alexis excused herself to freshen up in the ladies

room while Reginald ordered lunch. He exchanged pleasantries with the owner until Alexis returned. After the food arrived, they ate in silence for several minutes. The young actress found that she was quite hungry after all and she did feel much better after eating. She looked up from her plate as Reginald was taking his last bite of roast beef.

"How did you know I had been fired and that I was sitting on that bench? You couldn't have just happened along."

"Oh, that? I still have a few loyal friends working inside the studio. I had forgotten just how excellent these sandwiches are." He took a sip of his coffee. "So what are your plans now?"

"I don't really know." Her eyes misted over. "I'm out of work and I won't have a place to live unless I can find a job to pay the rent."

"Not to sound too negative, but you can bet Von Heller will do whatever he can to blackball your name," he said.

Her expression went from sad to angry. "I can't leave town until I find out what really happened to Lillian. Would you mind terribly if I moved in with you?"

"Surely you must be joking, right?" Reginald laughed nervously.

"No, I'm dead serious Reggie," she stared.

"Now Alexis, really. I have always lived alone. I have never gone for that sort of lifestyle," Reginald folded his arms across his chest.

"Well, I'm not asking you to sleep with me." Several heads turned their way.

"Quiet please," he whispered. "Are you trying to completely destroy my career?"

"What career Reggie? Besides, this is Hollywood. Nobody cares who lives with who."

"Whom," he corrected.

She gave him a sharp kick.

Murder By Plane 27.

Reginald pointed his index finger and clumsily attempted to change the subject.

"What did you find in the file room that was so secretive it resulted in your termination?"

"I won't tell you until you agree to let me move in with you for awhile."

"How long is awhile?"

"Just until I get a job and we find out what really happened in that plane crash."

"That could take months."

"Don't you want to find out what happened?"

"I suppose so and that is why I have hired a detective."

"Who is this guy?"

"His name is Frank Brogan. He was with the police at some point in his career, however, to be honest, he seemed rather dodgy to me."

"That's why we need to look into this ourselves Reggie. If I can just have a room at your house for a little while we can work on this together. It's important." Reginald leaned back and gazed at her through half closed eyes.

"Hmm, I don't know. You can be very annoying at times. Now tell me what was in the file."
She shook her head and smiled. "Nope. Not until you agree to room and board."

"Good grief. Oh, all right, but only until you find a job and your own place or go back to Kansas."

"I'm not from Kansas." he was ready for the kick and caught her foot with his hand.

Reginald wanted to go home to his usual afternoon drink and then send the girl and Dominic with the car, but she had insisted they go straight over to retrieve her few personal belongings. She finally told him what she had seen in Lillian's file as they drove to his house.

28. T.E.Avery

"That does not surprise me in the least. I always knew Von Heller was a control nut," Reginald stated.

"I only had time to read a few lines, but what I saw was slanderous and most certainly not true."

"Bruno keeps that trash on file so he can use it to blackmail his stable of stars. If anyone gets out of line he just tells them he will release something to the press and ruin their careers."

"How awful. Did he ever try that with you?"

"I live such a boring life he could never get anything on me."

She laughed at the joke and he suddenly realized how gorgeous she looked with her hair blowing in the breeze as his flashy automobile streaked down the beach road. Dominic waited just inside when they walked through the front entrance.

"Hi boss. Miss Moxley. There was a phone call for you boss. A private eye. He say you should call him back on account of he got important news for you."

"Did he say what it was about?"

"No boss. He not say."

"Please take Miss Moxley's things into the spare bedroom. She will be staying here for the time being. And show her where everything is," Reginald instructed.

"Yes boss," Dominic tried not to smile.

"And get that smirk off of your face. She just needs a place to stay for awhile."

"Yes boss," Dominic grinned.

Alexis followed the big Italian through the house while Reginald went into the study.
He poured himself a small glass of vintage cognac, picked up the phone and asked the operator to connect him with the detective's number.

After Alexis settled into the spare room, she found Reginald seated at his desk in the study. An empty glass was nearby.

"Did the detective have anything useful that might help us?" she asked.

"I think he has actually stumbled onto something. It seems he has found a probable witness to the possible sabotage."

"Really?" she asked excitedly and sat in one of the leather chairs.

"Would you like a drink?" he asked.

"No. Just tell me what that detective found?"

"Well, it's not much really. He found a chap who was a security guard at the studio when the accident occurred. He said there is a good chance this guard saw someone sneaking around the hanger the night before the crash."

"Oh my gosh. Reggie. Then it was sabotage."

"We still cannot be sure of that yet Alexis."

"But why would someone be sneaking around that hanger?"

"There are quite a number of other reasons. Theft for one."

"It's too much of a coincidence," she shook her head.

"I instructed Brogan to talk to the security cop and find out everything he remembered seeing that night. This is all we can do for now."

"Yeah, I suppose you must be right," she sounded disappointed. "I'll take that drink now."

He poured her a small cognac and another for himself and took a seat in the other pub chair. "Cheers."

"Cheers," she replied without enthusiasm and took a sip. "What about those files we were discussing earlier? Can we get our hands on them?"

"What do you mean?"

"We can't just let that goon keep all that trash about my sister, Reggie."

"Yes, I hate it too." He seemed to be deep in thought.

"Well, what can we do to get those files?" she asked.

"What you are asking is not an easy task Alexis. I will need to discuss our legal options with my lawyer."

"I was thinking about going in there and taking the darn files," she announced, after being fortified by a second cognac. "Oh, I see. And how would you manage to achieve your objective?" he said with amusement.

"I would sneak right in there when nobody was around and just grab the files."

"You already tried that, remember?"

"But not at night. I could sneak in …."

"No Alexis. That is all you need. Breaking and entering."

"I didn't say I was going to break anything. I was just going to sneak in and …."

"No. No. No. You cannot sneak in. You would be caught and prosecuted."

"What do you suggest we do then?"

"We won't do anything. I will discuss this with my attorney in the morning. Perhaps he can use some legal apparatus or something."

"Or something?" she said with a slight slur.

"Do you like the cognac? It is very old and rare, like me."

"I like it better than you," she said playfully as she peeked over the top of the glass.

"Me too." He finished his drink.

Greta came to the door and announced supper was ready.

"You go ahead, I need to call my lawyer and set up an appointment for tomorrow. I was planning on drinking vast quantities of scotch later and I don't want to forget."

"You drink too much Reggie." She stumbled on her way out.

"Look who's talking" he called after her.

The next day Reginald greeted his old friend, Max Carver, with an eager hand shake and a smile. Alexis had insisted on coming with him, but had second thoughts upon viewing the lawyer's cramped and stuffy office. She noticed it had a shabby appearance with one inexpensive desk lamp and overhead bare light bulb.

Murder By Plane 31.

The place reeked of stale cigarettes and there was a trace of some type of cheap cologne.

"It has been ages since we've last seen each other Max."

"Yeah, it has Reg. We'll have to schedule some time to have a drink and catch up on things." He came around his desk with a noticeable limp. "Who is this lovely young lady?" The way he looked her over gave Alexis the creeps.

"This is Alexis Moxley. She is Lillian's sister. She moved here from the Midwest several months ago."

"Hello Alexis. I'm sure we must have met at your sister's funeral. I only knew your sister through Reg, but she seemed to be a wonderful young lady. You look so much like her that you could be her twin."

"Thank you Mr. Carver."

"Please, call me Max. Everyone does."

There was that smarmy smile again, Alexis thought.

"Okay Max," she tried to smile back.

"How is that private detective working out for you Reg?" Carver motioned for them to take a seat.

Reginald continued the conversation. "I must admit I was not very impressed with Mr. Brogan in the beginning, however, he seems to think he has found a witness that may have seen something,"

"What? Well, that's great," Carver said.

"Brogan is still trying to track the witness down to obtain the information. He should be speaking to him any day now."

"I certainly hope the lead works out for you Reg. I've always thought it was just a tragic accident myself," the lawyer stated.

"I thought so too Max, but the police report originally said possible sabotage and now Brogan has discovered a witness. We are hoping it works out too. Thank you for advising me to use Mr. Brogan."

"Don't mention it Reg. You said something in our phone conversation about some slanderous files you

32. T.E.Avery

wanted to recover. What was that all about?"

Reginald leaned forward and explained everything about the scandalous reports kept by Von Heller and how Alexis had been terminated for searching for them.

Carver turned to Alexis. "They fired you for going into the file closet?"

"Well, it was a little more than just going into the file room. Those files were classified and we were told not to go into that area," she added sheepishly.

"Where do I come in?" the lawyer asked.

"We want to get our hands on those files. There could be important evidence concerning our case. Can we take some sort of legal action to seize them?"

"We could try, but I'll be honest with you both. We probably stand a snowball's chance in hell of getting those files."

"Would it really be that difficult Max?" Reginald asked.

"Von Heller is one of the most powerful men in Hollywood. He has half the judges in town in his vest pocket."

"I suppose there is not much to be done then," Reginald turned to Alexis.

"What do you mean?" she said angrily.

"What Reginald means, Alexis, is there is no legal way to obtain those papers. What evidence are you looking for, if I may ask?"

"The reports in those files may lead us to the person responsible for causing the crash that killed my sister Mr. Carver."

"Are you trying to say there is real evidence in those files that could point out an individual who sabotaged the plane?"

"I didn't get very far when I was reading them, before being caught, but I think it would be beneficial to have another look."

"I see what you mean, young lady, but I'm afraid there just isn't anything I can do. I'm very sorry." He shook his head.

"I think we should find a way to get in there and take those files," Alexis said.

"I can't be part of anything illegal Reg. Not even for you," the lawyer said.

"She doesn't mean it Max. Alexis is just a trifle angry at the moment."

"I'm mad all right and I want those files. You do too Reggie."

"We would like to acquire those files by legal means Max. Are you sure it is impossible?"

"I'm positive Reg. I can't help you with this one old buddy," Carver shrugged.

"Thank you for your advice Max and we will have that drink soon."

The two ex-flyers shook hands and Reginald took Alexis by the elbow to lead her out. Reginald observed a storm of emotions brewing on her face as they exited the lawyer's office.

"I can't believe you just gave up so easily Reggie. I feel like kicking you."

"Go ahead and kick me if it makes you feel better, but I have not yet given up."

"You haven't? What do you mean?"

"No, I just didn't want Max to hear us talking about breaking and entering."

"You're kidding, right?" her eyes widened.

"No, I am quite serious. Are you ready for lunch?"

Back at Reginald's house, Greta prepared their lunch and they ate on the patio under the awning. The heat would have been unbearable, if not for the Pacific breeze. Reginald refused to discuss their plans until they had eaten and could retire to the privacy of the study. He poured two brandies once they were sequestered in the small room.

34. T.E.Avery

"This is much better for conferring on our nefarious undertaking."

"Wow, you make it sound so wicked. Do you think we're doing the right thing?"

"It is not necessarily wrong if you are fighting against evil."

"Did you learn that in the war?"

"That and much more," he said with a sad expression.

They made themselves comfortable in the soft leather chairs.

"Now will you tell me your plan?"

"I have been giving it some thought, Kansas," he said

"Not that nickname again?" She rolled her eyes. "What's your plan smart guy?"

"We go in under the cover of darkness."

"And?" Long pause. "And?" She asked again.

"That is all I have been able to come up with so far." Reginald scratched his head.

"You can't be serious?"

"Not entirely, but I still must work out all of the details before I just blunder in and get myself arrested."

"What do you mean by all of this "I" and "myself" business?"

"I will go in while you wait in the car," he smiled.

"No. Absolutely not, boyo."

"Technically I still work at the studio and could present some sort of explanation for my late night visit, but you, on the other hand, have been recently terminated."

"I don't want to wait in the car," she said with a pout.

"Sorry, but it is the only way. Stiff upper lip. That's the girl." He patted her hand.

"Do you know how to find the file closet?" Alexis fluttered her eyelashes.

"Well, er… ah. Not exactly, but I shouldn't have too much trouble finding it."

"You can't get in and out quickly without my help Reggie."

He hesitated for a moment. "You may have a good point, even if I hate to admit it."

"So I get to go in with you?"

"Yes, but we have to disguise you," he said.

"So the security goons won't recognize me if we are seen?"

"Exactly, my girl."

"How will we get in so late at night? I'm sure everything will be locked up."

"It just so happens that I have a key that will open any door in town," he said with enthusiasm.

"What kind of key can do that?"

"A special key," he said in a conspiratorial hush and walked over to the desk. Reginald opened a hidden compartment and took out a small black key.

"What's so special about that? It looks like an ordinary little key to me," she asked.

"I acquired it many years ago, in Paris, during the war. I have found it to be of use from time to time."

"Are you sure it will work Reggie?"

"Yes, I am certain it will open any lock in the studio, my girl."

"So we go over there tonight and try out your key? You better slow down on that brandy."

"No. He poured another drink. We will have to cover our alibis during the time we are breaking into the studio."

"What do you mean?"

"We should be seen together, in public and by a lot of people, close to the time when we are making off with the files."

"But how? I thought we would just drive over and get in and out," she said.

"We will get in and out after we make an appearance at the premier of Von Heller's new film.

36. T.E.Avery

It will be showing at the Chinese theater just down the street from the studio."

"You mean that new horror film?"

"That's the one, my girl."

"Is "my girl" my new nickname?"

"No, I just feel generous tonight, Kansas," he replied with a wink.

"I really should kick you, but I'm feeling generous tonight too," she said with a smile at the corner of her mouth.

Chapter 4.

Frank Brogan shambled into his shabby, one bedroom, flat which served as both living quarters and an office. Brogan switched on the radio and poured himself a glass of cheap Irish whiskey. He sat in a tattered armchair to listen to the news broadcast and think about the days events.

  Brogan had called Reginald St. John to tell him about a possible witness he found by chance and had, of course, elaborated and embellished the story to impress the movie star. He told Reginald he had been scanning the city for possible leads, but in truth, he had been wetting his whistle in a favorite pub, when his luck changed. "Luck of the Irish," he laughed aloud.

  Brogan had tried finding out who the security people were on the night before the accident, but his contact with the police said the studio never fully cooperated and no one had come forward willingly. He then tried inquiring around town about anyone who might know someone who worked at the studio at the time of the airplane crash a year ago.

  The bartender, at this particular gin mill, knew of a woman who came in sometimes, whose ex-husband had worked at Fairmont Studios less than a year ago. She had kicked her old man out after an all night drunken brawl because he had lost his night watchman job at the studio. The bartender said the guy was now unemployed and homeless. He had become just another forgotten man on the streets of the city.

  Brogan talked to the ex-wife, and after providing her with a bottle of booze, had found that she knew a thing or two about the plane crash. She said her ex-husband had been working the late shift on the night before the airplane crash. She said her old man, who liked to be around airplanes, had worked with Glen Curtis on Long Island before the war and even knew how to fly. "Yeah right, "Brogan scoffed.

  She claimed the ex told her he had actually seen a person in the hanger and that he knew the intruder. Her

38. T.E.Avery

husband said he had called out to the person, who had then made a quick get away. He heard a car starting up and pulling away a short time later. Brogan called St. John that evening to relate the good news, but held back any pertinent names, just in case. After all, St. John could replace the detective with someone else.

Now he needed to track the witness down and get the entire story from the guy. He would have to do this the hard way. Tracking a hobo could be difficult and expensive. If Brogan padded the bill, he could make out like a bandit. He picked up a pencil and scrap of paper to scribble something down, eyes squinting to focus. He would go out later this evening to continue his search. Frank Brogan never gave up when money was involved. He knew, one way or another, this case would turn into something special for him.

Dominic followed Alexis into the house, arms loaded with packages. Alexis needed a new formal gown, and shoes, to attend the film premier with Reginald. He had sent her shopping that morning in the car driven by his loyal chauffeur. Reginald appeared from his office; pipe in hand, when he heard the side door open. He was dressed in a black satin house robe, comfortable slacks and loafers.

"Did you buy the entire store, Kansas?" Dominic nodded his head over the stack of boxes in his massive arms. "Yes boss."

"Oh, I didn't get that much really. Just an evening gown, a party dress, shoes and some accessories," Alexis said

"Is that all?" Reginald said with a chuckle.

"Hope you don't mind Reggie? You said to get whatever I thought I needed."

"No.no. Don't worry. We didn't have time to find a proper designer, so I am sure you did your best."

"I promise to pay you back. You know that, don't you?"

"Nevermind. It's only money," Reginald said.

Murder By Plane 39.

"Thanks Reggie. And thank you Dom." She gave them both a quick peck on the cheek, a bounce in her step as she walked away.

The two men looked at each other and shrugged.

Alexis found Reginald in his study that evening. He was sitting at his old rolltop desk typing away at something, his ever-present drink nearby. "Well, what do you think?"

With her hair dyed platinum blonde the resemblance to her sister was remarkable. His look of amazement was all too apparent.

"Are you okay? You don't like it do you?" She patted her hair self-consciously.

"I do... I do like it. It's just that the ...ah change caught me by surprise," he said.

"Isn't that the general idea?" Alexis fluttered her long lashes.

"Yes and I think it will work quite well," he said in a clipped tone. "Greta said she had prepared a dessert in the kitchen before she left. Why don't you go and have some? I am sure it must be delicious."

"What are you writing?"

"Oh, nothing really. Just some fiction," he said with some annoyance.

"What kind of fiction?"

"I had been dabbling in writing a screenplay some years ago, but have not done anything for a while. I thought I would give it a try again."

"Really? That's wonderful Reggie. What made you start writing again?"

"I don't know. I just sat down earlier today and started typing. Remarkable really."

She sat down and leaned back against the cool leather of the armchair. "I'm trying real hard to relax, but I feel so nervous about breaking into the studio."

"Perhaps a brandy would help?" he suggested.

"I'm afraid Reggie," she said.

"What are you afraid of? Is it breaking and entering

and the consequences or perhaps you are nervous about going to the premier. If you are afraid of meeting a multitude of movie stars, don't be. They are just a bunch of superficial snobs with inflated egos. If it is our mission you are nervous about you need not worry. We will be in and out in no time."

"Is that how you think of all of this? Is it like a mission in the war?"

He looked at her with a calm that she had not seen in him before. "Yes. It is our mission to find the truth."

"It's not that I'm afraid of what we are about to do, but that there may be a killer walking around free. What if we fail Reggie? What if we never find out what really happened?"

"Never say never. We will not know anything until we uncover more evidence. We need to get a look at those files. I talked to Brogan and he seems to think he is getting closer to finding the witness."

"He did? Why didn't you tell me?"

"I just did, besides, you and Dominic left before I was up this morning."

"Okay, so now we have a witness to the sabotage and maybe some incriminating evidence too," she said excitedly.

"Possible witness, only possible sabotage and maybe some scanty evidence."

"Pour a small glass of brandy for me please," she said.

Murder By Plane 41.

The advertisements touted the premier of the gothic thriller, The Evil Cat, as the best horror film ever produced. It pitted two of Hollywood's horror film greats, Adolf Bella and Boris Koffsky, together for the first time. Dominic pulled the Duesenberg alongside the curb and a female valet in a skimpy, black cat, costume immediately opened the door.

Reginald exited the car first, amid a tremendous roaring applause from the crowd. Flashes from the many photographers' cameras blinded them. After saluting the crowd, he turned to hand Alexis out of the backseat. Reginald could see her eyes widen with surprise and perhaps some fear, but she straightened her shoulders and waved to the crowd. There was another round of cheering and applause.

"Steady Kansas," Reginald almost shouted against her ear.

He was dressed in a black tuxedo with tails and sported a top hat. Alexis looked stunning in her new evening gown perfectly matching her green eyes and a pale mink cape around her bare shoulders. Her platinum hair was set in the popular short style. Her jeweled earrings and necklace sparkled in the cameras flashes. Reginald and Alexis created something of a sensation among the reporters who yelled questions at the dashing movie star. "Who's the dame Reggie?" "Where have you been hiding lately?" "Are you two married?"

A line of policemen were on hand to keep everyone back behind the ropes. Reginald and his lovely date walked arm in arm down the red carpet. They passed through the theater lobby and were shown to their seats by ushers in vampire outfits.

Reginald turned to Alexis and put his mouth close to her ear. "That went well."

"I've never seen so many movie stars in one place before," she gasped.

42. T.E.Avery

Reginald thought she sounded exactly like a little girl and he suddenly felt strangely protective. "I'm glad we decided to do this."

"Me too," she smiled and waved enthusiastically as several of Hollywood's biggest stars walked by.

"Let us not forget the importance of our mission my girl."

"You had to remind me," her smile faded.

"Enjoy yourself for now Alexis for no one knows what fate may bring our way."

She was so enraptured by the excitement of the moment she only heard the first part of what Reginald had said; the lights began to dim.

Alexis thought the film much too unrealistic to be enjoyed. The makeup was atrocious and the sets were very bogus. Besides, her mind kept drifting away as she went over their plans for later that night. A part of her mind kept screaming, "Stop. You're in danger. Don't be an idiot." The movie was a little more than an hour in length, but it seemed much longer.

After the lights came on everyone milled about in the lobby to drink champagne from crystal flutes and congratulating the actors, director, and writers and, of course, Mr. Bruno Von Heller.

She felt a, not too gentle, nudge against her ribs. "That is Von Heller over in the corner with his entourage. Let us say hello."

She looked across the lobby, but could barely see Von Heller's bald head through the crowd of fawning retainers around him. "Shouldn't we just try to slip out of here?"

"It is too late now Kansas. The evil spider has seen us." Reginald seemed to be enjoying himself.

"But Reggie ... I don't think ...." Alexis began.

"One of his toadies is coming our way now. This will be great fun," he chuckled.

Murder By Plane 43.

A primly dressed female walked straight up to Reginald. "Mr. St. John?"

"I think you probably know who I am," he said crisply.

"Yes. Of course. Sorry. My boss, Mr. Von Heller, has asked me to invite you over."

"Over where?"

"Over to his side of the lobby sir."

"All right then. Come along Alexis." She put her hand on his extended arm and together they walked over to Von Heller's corner.

Alexis thought it was appropriate that Von Heller was dressed all in black. He had elevated himself above everyone by climbing onto a wicker-throne-chair that had been set atop a small platform. "Evil fat spider," she whispered.

Bruno Von Heller was a small fat man with a bald head and not a single redeeming feature or quality. Alexis almost recoiled when she set eyes on the repulsive figure. She immediately perceived his base nature as if it were a palpable odor wafting toward her. This is the enemy, she thought.

"Hello Reginald. How are you old friend?" Alexis noticed his slight accent.

"Hello Bruno," Reginald replied coolly.

"You must introduce me to your gorgeous young companion, Reginald," Bruno said.

"This is Alexis Moxley. She is the sister of Lillian Livingston."

A small measure of shock registered on the fat man's face. "Of course it is. I can now see the resemblance. It is good to meet you, my dear." He reached out to take her hand.

Alexis wanted to kick him repeatedly or run away as quickly as she could, but she stood her ground. "Hello Mr. Von Heller," she said in a small voice, her vocal cords and stomach tightening.

Von Heller turned to Reginald and inquired in a

44. T.E.Avery

condescendingly polite tone about his recent film career. Reginald shrugged off the insult with his parry. "So Bruno, I see you have decided to produce second rate horror movies."

There was an audible gasp from the group encircling them.

"I only create the best quality films." Von Heller's eyes had narrowed to thin slits.

Alexis wanted to laugh, but managed to control her mirth.

"It was all I could do to watch the entire movie Bruno." Reginald shook his head.

"I only select the most proficient actors. You obviously cannot appreciate fine art."

"The actors were fine Bruno, but you should have spent more on writers and set design. The whole thing was a disaster."

"That is your opinion, Mr. Reginald St. John." Von Heller's face was now red and his expression so full of malice that Alexis felt her blood turn to ice. "I will see you again Reginald. Miss Moxley." He curtly bowed his head to dismiss the two.

"Goodnight Bruno. And good luck with that little film of yours."

They exited the lobby as fast as they could manage, attracting attention from other attendees. Reginald reached out to take two glasses of champagne from a waiter's tray.

"This stuff is not half bad, really," he said.

"You weren't half bad yourself Reggie. I thought we would have to fight our way out of that creepy place."

"I was beginning to think so too. Here, have a drink."

They were unaware of the small dark car parked across the street from the Chinese theater and the person observing them from the driver's seat.

Dominic opened the car door as soon as he saw

Reginald and Alexis nearly running from the entrance. As Reginald slipped into the backseat beside Alexis he just had time to spy the dark, little coupe speeding away. It seemed strangely familiar to him, but he let it pass from his thoughts.

"Let's get ourselves over to the studio quickly Dominic."

"Okay boss. We on the way now."

The art deco façade loomed over them in the darkness as they approached the studio along the boulevard. Dominic turned onto a narrow side alley and drove slowly toward the backlots. This is where most of the filming had been done since the days of silent pictures. Movie sets could be seen skulking in the darkness.

An old aircraft hanger, used for storage and mechanical repairs, was positioned between the lane and a small runway. The studio used Van Nuys Airport for any real aerial requirements on, or off, camera.

A large car suddenly appeared out of the darkness and hurtled at them with amazing speed as they moved along the diminutive road. Dominic skillfully horsed the Duesenberg out of the way just in time. They all exchanged startled looks.

"What you want to do now boss? Keep going or turn back?"

"I think we should continue. What do you think Alexis?"

"What if they call security, or the police, and catch us breaking in?"

"The way that car left here makes me doubt they have any intention of involving the police. They must have been up to no good."

"Who do you think it could have been Reggie?"

"I don't know, but I'm sure it must have been something illegal. Hopefully the studio cops were not alerted by the sound of the car speeding away."

"So we go on boss?"

46. T.E.Avery

"Let's go Dominic," Reginald said firmly.

They parked behind the aircraft hanger. Reginald gave Dominic instructions to stay in the car and keep watch.

"If anyone approaches you may have to make up some sort of story as to why you are parked back here. I am sure you will be able to handle that all right."

"Okay boss," Dominic nodded.

A high wooden fence surrounded the entire area, but the rear half of the hanger was not within the enclosure. They went to the back of the building and found a locked door.

"Why do you want to go through here Reggie?"

"Because I am quite familiar with this hanger and I want to have a look around."

Reginald used his special key to unlock the sturdy wooden door.

"What do you know? It really works."

"You mean you didn't know if it would work?"

"Just a joke," he whispered.

Reginald pulled a flashlight from his pocket and stepped into the darkened hanger first. "Keep close and do not stray," he continued to whisper.

"Don't worry about me. I'm sticking like glue." She grabbed one of his jacket tails and followed him inside.

Reginald felt his chest tighten, for there was his old Nieuport biplane looking as beautiful as ever in the glow of moonlight streaming through a skylight overhead. It had been completely restored to its original condition after being almost totally destroyed in the crash a year ago.

"Is this one of your stunt planes Reggie? It's gorgeous."

"Yes, the very one that killed your sister I am sorry to say."

"But, how can you tell? It could be a different plane."

"I would know that airplane anywhere."

Murder By Plane 47.

Alexis felt her knees buckle. "It looks almost ghostly in the moonlight. Like a lovely phantom."

"It's just an airplane. Nothing more. Let's have a closer look and then we will continue on with our task," he said.

As they walked closer to the rear of the Nieuport, Reginald could see something was off. The port side wing seemed to be slanting downward. They made their way around the tail section. Reginald placed a hand on the fuselage and ran it along the smooth fabric as if inspecting the old biplane before a flight.

He stopped suddenly, his head moving sharply as he spotted something. He turned around quickly to face Alexis.

"Do not go any further. I think there is a body lying under the plane," he said.

"Are you sure?" Alexis asked in a shaky voice.

"Just stay back here and do not touch anything," he said quietly. Reginald walked to the lower wing and bent down carefully. He could see there was indeed a body pinned beneath the undercarriage as he pointed the beam of his flashlight under the plane. After several minutes he returned to the spot where Alexis had planted herself. She was leaning against the side of the airplane and looking pale.

"Are you all right Alexis?"

"I think so. Is it really a dead body?"

"Yes, it is Frank Brogan."

"That detective you hired? But how?"

"I am afraid so. It seems he has met with an untimely demise."

"What do you mean?" She felt herself getting nauseous.

"I mean that someone killed him and put his body under the wheel."

"We have to call the police Reggie."

"Not until we accomplish what we intended to do tonight."

48. T.E.Avery

"Well, we better be quick about it then."

"Yes, let's get out of here," he said.

Alexis felt her legs trembling as they made their way around the plane and toward the front of the building. They found a side door ajar and slipped through it after a careful look outside. Walking slowly along the fence, they noticed a small gate left open.

"This must be how he got in and through the side door in the hanger."

"Frank Brogan?" She asked.

"And his murderer. That must have been the killer's car that almost hit us as he was fleeing the scene."

"Now I'm scared Reggie," she said through chattering teeth.

"Would you rather go back to the car?"

"No. You need me to find the storeroom."

"All right then. Quickly now."

The scene was almost surrealistic with the two actors, dressed in formal gown and tuxedo; sneaking along the wooden fence by moonlight. The thought occurred to them both; what would a policeman say if they were discovered?

Chapter 5.

Reginald used his skeleton key to unlock a back door he knew would lead into the offices of the vast building. He and Alexis followed a long dark hallway past many closed doors. They had been on the studio property for a little over fifteen minutes, but it felt more like hours to them both.

"This is where you come in, my girl," Reginald said in a low voice.

Alexis took the lead as they walked through the warrens of dim corridors. Even in such a tense situation, not knowing if any one of the hall doors would open at any minute, Reginald could not help noticing her incredible shape in the tight fitting gown. He reminded himself mentally of their reason for being here. He must look through those files and find any evidence, if there was any.

He wondered if it was worth the risk they were taking and his thoughts went back to the hanger and Brogan's limp form shoved under the biplane. Why was Brogan in the hanger and who could have killed the P. I.? That had to have been the murderer driving away, almost running them down as they approached the rear of the hanger.

They were about to turn a corner when Alexis stopped short and held up her hand to keep him from speaking. They heard the voices of, at least, two men rapidly approaching. Reginald pushed Alexis against the wall. As quickly as possible, Reginald and Alexis turned and padded back the way they had come, zipping around a corner with no time to spare, judging by the sounds behind them. Reginald put his mouth to her ear. "I'll use my key."

They ducked into a dark office. Locking the door, they heard voices on the other side.

"That about does it for the rounds tonight. We got all night to take it easy now," one of the men said.

50. T.E.Avery

"Sounds good to me Ed. You still got that bottle stashed away somewhere?"

"Yeah, you got the cards?"

Reginald opened the door a crack, peeking out, when he heard the voices trailing off in the distance. "Quickly, while they are occupied."

Alexis led the way once more, around a corner and to the Personnel Department.

Reginald again used the skeleton key to let them in. Alexis walked across the dark room carefully to avoid tripping over office furniture. Reginald started to use his special key to unlock the storage room, but Alexis suddenly reached out and grabbed his arm.

"What is it?"

"Do you smell smoke?"

Reginald barely had to sniff the air to get a strong scent of acrid smoke.

"Yes, I smell it. Look at the bottom of the door."

Tendrils of smoke snaked under the door. He put his hand on the wood surface.

"Hot."

"That entire room is on fire Reggie. If we open the door.... "

"...We would become matchsticks. There is nothing more we can do here. Let's go," he said.

They fled the way they had come, through the building and out across the studio backlot, without incident. They exited through the open gate instead of the hanger. Dominic had positioned the Duesenberg facing out of the alley and waited beside the car. He saw them coming and jumped into the driver's seat to start the engine.

"Let's go Dominic. Quickly."

"We goin home now boss?"

"No. Find a police call box. We must hurry."

"Okay boss," Dominic stepped on the gas pedal.

Reginald used the nearest police call phone to report the fire and Brogan's body in the hanger.

Murder By Plane 51.

"Now let's find a party, and quickly, so we have an alibi for the last hour or so."

"But I'm in no mood to go to a party Reggie," Alexis blinked back tears.

"I know, my girl." He took her hand and gently massaged it. "But we must make it seem like we have just come from the theater."

The tires squealed as Dominic took a curve too sharply and Reginald had to reach out to steady the young actress.

"I suppose you're right, but nothing has worked out the way we planned. We didn't get the files, we found a dead man and we almost got burned alive. Oh Reggie." She buried her head into his shoulder and sobbed. He put his arm around her.

"Lets just forget about the party Dominic and head straight home. We will just have to take our chances."

"Okay boss. We go home now."

Dominic swung the car around in a tight turn and drove them in the direction of the Pacific coast and the sanctuary of Reginald's home.

"I no longer believe my plane crash was accidental. It seems to me that someone got to the studio before us to destroy the evidence and even commit murder to stop us discovering any other clues," Reginald said.

By the time they returned home, the young woman was at the point of exhaustion from the stress of the whole night's events. She still leaned against him, with eyes closed and brow furrowed, blocking out painful memories. Reginald knew the emotional toll had been greater than the physical. He helped Alexis into the cottage and to her room while Dominic parked the vehicle.

There was no one to help her remove the formal gown and he could see she would have difficulty in her present state. "Here, let me help," he said quietly.

She peered up at his face in the dim light to see whether

or not he was joking, but she could see only genuine concern. After her gown was unbuttoned and removed, she kicked off her shoes and fell onto the bed.

Reginald went into the nearby study and soon returned with two small glasses of brandy. "This will take the edge off a bit," he said, coming through the doorway, but when he looked at her lying on the bed he could see she was sound asleep. Covering her with a sheet, he bent down and kissed her pale forehead. He thought her face was angelic in slumber. Reginald returned to the study to down both glasses of brandy and to deal with his own emotional demons.

Reginald came downstairs, late, the next morning to find Alexis in the kitchen preparing breakfast for the two of them. She was wearing a navy blue blouse and pleated white skirt. It was the cook's day off and Alexis had decided to busy herself with domestic chores. He sat in one of the chrome, art deco, kitchen chairs without saying a word. Reginald could hear bacon crackling in a large iron skillet and it, along with the strong coffee brewing, smelled delicious.

"I haven't been tucked into bed since I was very young," she said over her shoulder.

"You were out for the count and needed help taking your gown off. I didn't know what to do, so I assisted you. I promise I was a perfect gentleman."

"Oh, I know. I didn't mean it like that," her voice sounded a little shaky.

"What did you mean?"

"I just thought it was very nice of you, that's all."

"Well, you did save me from possible injury last night by warning me about the fire before I blundered into that storeroom."

"I'm usually the one doing the blundering. I'm glad it was you for a change."

"Someone wanted us dead or in jail and out of the way it seems," he said.

"It looks that way to me too. I didn't know if you

would agree with me or not. Have you seen the front page yet?" She set a big plate of scrambled eggs and bacon down in front of him. His countenance seemed to lift at the sight of the food.

"This looks wonderful. Just what I needed after a long night of intrigue and murder," he picked up the newspaper and read the headline. FIRE AT FAIRMONT STUDIO.

"Please don't joke about it. I'm having a tough time getting it out of my mind."

"I'll have to call Max to let him know about Brogan's death. I should relate all of last night's events and get his advice."

"Do you really think you should Reggie?"

"Why not. He is my lawyer and a close friend. Anything I say to him will be in the strictest confidence."

"Maybe it was all just a series of accidents. What if Brogan died of heart failure?"

"That is very unlikely since the side of his head was bashed in. I think the police will find that the body was placed under the aircraft after his death."

"Maybe he fell and bumped his head after he had the heart attack."

"You did not see his head. The skull was crushed. That usually does not happen with a simple fall," Reginald took a bite of scrambled eggs and a sip of coffee.

"I see your point." She pushed her plate away. "I was just trying to play devil's advocate."

"Yes, but are you forgetting the fire that almost burned us to a crisp? He bit into a slice of bacon. "Or the car that nearly ran us down?"

"No, I'm not forgetting, but I wish I could."

"Thank you for preparing this sumptuous brunch. I cannot remember when I have had such a tasty meal." He gestured with his hand for emphasis.

"You didn't think I was going to move in here

without doing something for you in return, did you?"

"I really did not know you very well prior to the last few days. Just the few times we talked when you came to visit your sister."

"I really miss her," her eyes misted.

"I miss her too. I suppose that is one thing you and I share in common Alexis."

"How are we going to find out what really happened to her now? Are you going to hire another detective?"

"No. No more detectives," he said sternly.

"So, where do we start?"

"You were extremely upset by last night's events. Do you think it is in your best interest to continue being involved in this?"

"What do you mean? Are you trying to tell me to stay out of it Reggie?"

"You have been through an awful lot of stress lately with the loss of your job and rehashing all of the details surrounding Lillian's death. Not to mention all that occurred last night. Perhaps it would be best if I continue alone in the investigations."

"Well. I can't believe this. You are trying to shut me out. What if I had gone back to the car last night and had not been there to warn you about the fire? And I only got that job so I could snoop around. It meant nothing to me."

"Yes, I suppose you may be right, but I was only trying to protect you."

"I know you are Reggie." Her tone softened. "And I do appreciate all you've done for me, but I've got to find out who killed my sister."

That afternoon the two actors found themselves drawn to Reginald's cozy office to discuss the case. A ceiling fan twirled slowly above them sending a cool breeze down through the room. Reginald poured two glasses of chilled white wine. They sat in silence for several minutes sipping the refreshing beverage.

"The papers speculated that Brogan's death was an

accident. Do you think it might be a cover-up by the studio heads?" She asked.

"Yes, some sort of deliberate misinformation being spread around to the reporters, but the murder will eventually get into the papers, unless the police are involved in the cover- up somehow."

"What about the fire? I wonder if arson has been definitely determined yet?"

"Not according to the news in the papers or on the radio. I suppose that is being covered up by Von Heller and his goons too."

"So, what's the next move Reggie?"

"I think the only logical thing to do is locate the witness that Brogan was looking for."

"Hey, do you think that's why Brogan was murdered?"

"It is a very distinct possibility, but that would mean that the killer is trying to locate and eliminate the witness too."

"Yeah and you know what that means don't you?"

"Yes, I believe you have just answered your own question about our next move Kansas."

"I'm not from Kansas Reggie, besides, I thought I had a new nickname now?"

"The new one is only when I am feeling generous."

"Sometimes your accent makes you sound like you're from England," she laughed.

"Actually, I was born in England and brought up in New York."

"Aha, I thought so."

"But we should be getting back to our discussion concerning the case."

"Changing the subject are we? For such a big celebrity you are a man of mystery, Mr. St. John." Reginald noticed the slur in her speech.

Later that day Reginald received a call from Max Carver. The two former comrades talked about Brogan's death and the fire at the studio. The lawyer offered to find another detective to continue searching for the witness, but Reginald declined.

"Did Brogan give you the name of the witness Reg?" Carver asked.

"No, I am afraid he did not get that far Max. It looks like I'll have to start at the beginning."

"Well, good luck old buddy and please keep me posted."

"Of course. Goodbye Max," Reginald hung up the receiver.

Reginald found Alexis lounging in a lawn chair watching the sunset over the Pacific, scantily dressed in shorts and halter top.

"What a picture," he said.

"It's beautiful, isn't it?"

"Oh, you mean the sunset," he said with a lopsided grin. "Yes, this view is one of the reasons I bought the place."

"It's the perfect setting. I could stay here forever," she added wistfully.

"Forever?" Reginald gulped.

"Relax Reggie. I didn't really mean permanently. I'd like my own place one day; when I'm a star."

"I hope your dreams come true for you," he sat in a nearby chair and tried to keep his eyes from lingering on her legs.

"Did you find out anything more about the witness?"

"Max Carver called, but he didn't know anymore than we do. He asked me if I had found out anything from Brogan before he was killed. We shall have to start searching for this fellow from the few leads we have so far."

"What leads do we have?"

"Not many, I'm afraid. We must find the ex-wife that Brogan found out about. We should be able to coerce her to tell us any information she has about the whereabouts of this witness."

"And this witness, whoever he is, can tell us what, or

who, he saw the night before your plane crash. But how do we find his ex-wife if we don't have any names?"

"The same place that Brogan did I suppose."

"Where would that be Reggie?"

"A place where neither one of us will feel very comfortable, my girl."

"Oh, now you must be feeling generous again."

The bar was in a long low building with peeling gray paint and grimy windows, in the seediest part of town; one of many taverns that had sprung up after prohibition was repealed the year before. Reginald and Alexis had decided to try to keep a low profile by riding in a cab to this area of the city and Frank Brogan's apartment.

Reginald had let them in with his skeleton key only to find the place cleaned out, most likely by the owners, except for a matchbox with the name of a saloon crudely stamped on it.

As Reginald and Alexis walked to the ugly front door of the local bar, a hot dry wind kicked up a swirl of dust around them. They had dressed down for this outing so as not to appear overly conspicuous. Alexis wore one of her plain dresses and sensible flat soled shoes. Reginald dressed in khaki trousers, a brown shirt and fedora. They were still a striking couple and drew instant attention when they entered the dark smoky drinking establishment.

Reginald touched the small of her back, protectively, and steered them toward a vacant table. They both looked around as discreetly as possible still trying not to attract any interest.

"I will go to the bar and order us something to drink. Perhaps I can strike up a conversation with the bartender. Will you be okay here?"

"I think so," she looked around apprehensively.

"There aren't too many people in here."

"Just a few fellows playing pool and drinking beer."

58. T.E.Avery.

"They look pretty rough to me. Please don't stay gone too long."

"What if I kiss you passionately so they will think that we are more than friends?"

"Will you just go? And make it quick."

"Here I go. Suppose I just peck you on the cheek?"

"Go," she dismissed him with a wave of her hand.

"Don't get testy, my girl," he bent over and kissed her on the lips. There, that should suffice."

Reginald walked over to the bar where two old men were sitting on stools talking quietly.

They both looked up as Reginald approached. "Hey there son, can ya spare two bits for an old codger ta have a beer?"

Reginald got the bartenders attention and ordered four beers. Two for the old men and one each for he and Alexis.

"Thanks son, you're the first man to buy me a beer in a long time," the old man slurred and peered at Reginald through yellow watery eyes.

"Don't mention it. Maybe you could help me find someone."

"Like who, son?"

Reginald noticed the severe lack of teeth in the man's mouth and the copious amounts of spittle spewing forth as he spoke.

"I do not yet have a name, but her ex-husband worked at the Fairmont Studios as a security guard and it has recently come to my attention she may frequent this tavern."

The two wizened geezers looked from Reginald to each other and burst into wet laughter, which quickly turned into hacking coughs. "You sure do talk fancy son," the first old man said after recovering from his coughing attack.

"Thank you. Do you think you might know this woman or her husband?"

"What's the name again son?"

"I do not have a name or description, as I related earlier, however, her husband worked at Fairmont for a time," Reginald said.

"Let me think. Maybe another cold one will help me remember son," he said as he scratched his arm pit.

"Oh, alright, but first the name." Reginald was beginning to lose patience.

"Fisk," the old man sprayed.

Reginald attempted, as discretely as possible, to wipe his face. "Excuse me?"

"Fisk, that's her name son. Fisk, yeah. Now how about another cold one."

"First name old timer?" he suddenly realized the two men were probably only ten years older than he.

"Ah, let me think. Gladys Fisk. That's her name alright. Now how bout those beers?"

Reginald handed over the two beers he had ordered for Alexis and himself earlier. "Do you know where this Mrs. Fisk resides?"

"Huh?"

"Do you know where she lives?"

Another long pause while the disheveled old man took a long drink of the foamy beverage. "Ahhh, I think she stays a couple a blocks from here."

"Do you know the direction?"

"Out the front door and turn left," he pointed with a crooked finger.

"I don't suppose you would know the name of her ex-husband?"

Reginald realized, by the glazed expression in the old man's eyes, that he would not be getting more information. "Right." He called to the barman for more beer.

"Thanks for the beer son. You come back and see me anytime, yahear."

"Thank you. You have been a great help." Reginald turned from the bar only to see that Alexis was in trouble.

Chapter 6.

Three, tough looking, troublemakers had partially surrounded the table where Alexis still sat. One of them held a pool cue.

"Excuse me, but we were just leaving," Reginald said as he stepped over to the table.

Alexis tried to stand when she heard Reginald's voice, but one of the toughs crowded her and she could not get out of her chair. "What took you so long Reggie?"

"Back off now and allow the lady to stand, that's a good fellow."

"That's a good fellow," the largest one mocked.

Reginald pushed the giant out of the way. He anticipated the pool cue coming even before the other drunk had swung it. Reginald quickly grabbed a chair to block the expected blow. The stick broke in two as it struck the raised chair and Reginald caught the smaller piece. Wielding the cue like a sword Reginald jabbed the biggest thug in the gut, sending him down. The man with the other half of the broken cue swung it down in an arc, which Reginald easily parried. This was followed by a quick strike to the wrist, which made the ruffian cry out in pain and drop his stick. He was felled by a blow to the side of the neck. This left only one rough looking drunk who was moving in, from behind Reginald.

"Watch out Reggie." Alexis screamed. She jumped onto the thug's back, grabbing hold of his thin, greasy hair and an ear. The man howled in pain. Reginald spun around with his makeshift sword raised to strike.

"Don't hit me Reggie." Alexis yelled.

Reginald rammed the stick into the man's upper abdomen. The brute fell on his face with Alexis still on his back. Reginald could see the fight was gone from all three drunken toughs. He took Alexis by the hand to help her up.

"I told you we should have kissed passionately, Kansas," he joked.

Leaving quickly, they could hear the bartender yell.

Murder By Plane 61.

"Hey, I know who that is. That's Reginald St. John, the movie star."

Reginald and Alexis turned left after exiting the bar, as instructed by the old man.

The two were closely observed from across the street, but had no idea as they walked down the dirty sidewalk littered with broken bottles and old newspapers.

"I don't like being in this neighborhood after dark Reggie."

"I do not like it either, but we must, at least, find out where Mrs. Fisk lives. Even if she is not at home today, we can always come back to speak with her. But if the killer is out there trying to cover up his trail, it is urgent we talk to the woman and at least warn her of the danger," he replied.

"How did you learn to fight like that?"

"You said that you've seen my movies. I am, you know, one of the best swordsmen in Hollywood." He still held the broken pool cue and flourished it through the air like a fencing epee.

"Well, it's a good thing for us that you got your hands on that stick before one of those hoodlums did," Alexis added.

"I agree with you on that, my girl. Now, where do you think Mrs. Fisk's apartment would be located?"

They looked around in bewilderment at the rows of dilapidated buildings in one of the oldest sections of town.

"Maybe we should start knocking on doors and asking people if they know where she lives?" Alexis asked.

"That is an excellent idea." Reginald tossed the stick into a nearby shrub. They chose a rundown house to start their inquiries. Reginald knocked on the door loudly and they waited for what seemed a long time.

He rapped again, this time, even louder.

"Maybe it's time for us to go Reggie."

"No, wait. I think I hear footsteps approaching."

62. T.E.Avery

They noticed movement in the small window close to the door and after a few minutes it creaked open, just enough, that they could see a wrinkled face and filmy eyes peering out at them. They could not determine if it was a male or female.

"What do you want?" an old voice croaked.

"Good evening I ...."

"It's past my bedtime young man."

"I am sorry to bother you, but we are looking for someone who resides in this neighborhood."

"Are you with the police?"

"No. We are not with the police. We only want to locate a Mrs. Gladys Fisk. Do you know where her home is?"

"Why are you wantin to find her? Are ya kin?"

"It is a matter of personal business. Do you know Mrs. Fisk?"

"I didn't say if I knew her or not, but I might."

Reginald glanced over at Alexis and took out his wallet. "Would this help jog your memory?"

He handed over a five. A wrinkled and spotted claw snatched it with surprising speed.

"Thank you, sir. An old woman can use all the help she can get these days."

"Yes, I know what you mean my dear lady. Now, do you know where Mrs. Fisk resides?"

"Yeah, she stays just across the street in that tenement house over there. First floor."

She slammed the door shut and they heard the loud click of a bolt slide into place.

"What a charming neighborhood," Reginald stated sarcastically with a wave of his hand.

The residence across the narrow street was never a real house, but seemed to have been thrown together from scraps of demolished older buildings. It appeared to lean to one side. Reginald rapped on the door of the lower level apartment. He continued to pound on the cracked surface until his knuckles were sore.

Murder By Plane 63.

"She is obviously not at home this evening and, as we have just come from the bar she frequents, I would say she is either at work or visiting someone."

"A very shrewd deduction, my dear Sherlock," Alexis said.

"Are you mocking me? That is not very nice young lady." He held up his index finger.

"I'm not making fun of you Reggie, it's just that you sound so formal sometimes. You always seem to be so very proper."

"If you say so, Kansas. He said with a smirk. We should try upstairs and see if anyone is at home."

They walked up the short flight of stairs and knocked on the door to the dwelling that occupied the upper floor. The door was flung open by a surly man in his mid-fifties.

"Why are you bangin on people's doors this time of night?" He was bald headed and dressed in pants and a dirty undershirt, a crumpled newspaper under one arm.

"Excuse me, but do you know the lady who resides in the apartment below?"

The man was taken off guard by Reginald's good manners and accent. The bald man's rude demeanor softened somewhat.

"Yeah, I guess I know her, but she ain't what you would call a lady," he laughed.

"Do you know her ex-husband?" Reginald asked expectantly.

"Never did meet him. They fought like cats and dogs though. I heard em. She kicked him out one night, I think. Now she's with another guy. He's some kind of mechanic."

"Would you know where Mrs. Fisk is at present or where she works? It is extremely important."

"Important to you maybe, but not to me."

Reginald took out his wallet and held up a five dollar bill. "Does this increase the importance to you, sir?"

The man's eyes widened at the sight of the five. "I could use a five spot alright."

"First the information please," Reginald replied.

"Gladys works over at Fairmont. She's on the night shift custodial crew."

"Gladys Fisk works at Fairmont Studios?" Reginald looked back at Alexis who had been standing quietly behind him.

"That's what I said buddy." The man grabbed the five and slammed the door in their faces before Reginald could turn back around.

"That would fit. I'll bet she met her husband at Fairmont," Alexis said.

"You could be right, now we just need to find Gladys."

"Should we go to Fairmont?"

"I do not think that would be advisable at this time of night. We will come back here tomorrow and have a real talk with Mrs. Fisk."

They started down the stairs. When they reached the bottom, and turned a corner, Alexis let out a gasp as she was pulled by rough hands. The thugs from the bar had followed them. The two bigger ones grabbed Reginald by the arms while the smaller one pressed Alexis against the wall.

"Reggie." She struggled to free herself from her putrescent breathed attacker.

Reginald wished he had held onto that broken pool cue. The two toughs threw him to the ground. "Payback time pal," the big one snarled.

Reginald concentrated on warding off their kicks and punches while desperately trying to kick them in any area he could do some damage. The odds were not in his favor. Alexis turned her head away from the awful reek of the smallest of the three thugs.

"You creep. Let go."

"Shuddup girly," he raised his hand as if to strike her. Alexis instinctively closed her eyes and waited for the blow to come. Suddenly, he was pulled away by a great force. She heard the small man scream in pain. Alexis opened her eyes to witness him being thrown through the air like a rag doll and hitting the ground with a thud. She saw a hulking shadowy figure pull both men away from Reginald, giving them each a backhanded slap across the face. Dominic had come to their rescue just in time.

The smaller attacker had picked himself up and ran down the street as fast as he could go. His friends were both unconscious after a pounding from the big Italian.

"What took you so long Dominic?" Reginald was sitting up and turned to look up at Alexis. "Are you all right, my girl?"

"I'm okay, just a little shook up," she said in a shaky voice.

"You okay boss?" Dominic offered Reginald a hand up.

"I am bruised a little, but otherwise in tolerable condition."

"I want to get away from here now Reggie," Alexis said.

"Mala spina." Dominic spat at the two fallen thugs. He gave them one last contemptuous glare before climbing into the car.

Once they were in the car, Alexis lightly touched Reginald's swollen cheek. "We need to put ice on that. Did you tell Dominic to come and look for us?"

"We had an arrangement something like that, and he arrived at just the right time too."

"I'll say. All I want to do is get home and take a hot shower. Those men were horrible."

"I can agree with you on that, my girl. We will have to continue our investigation in the light of day."

The elegant Duesenberg looked thoroughly out of place as it cruised by the decrepit tenements and gin mills of the shabby neighborhood.

It was after midnight by the time they were home and

66. T.E.Avery

comfortably seated in the leather chairs of Reginald's den. Each had showered in their respective bathrooms and now wore long silk robes with oriental patterns. They were sipping twelve year old brandy from large crystal snifters. Dominic had retired to his own apartment.

"You took quite a beating tonight. How do you feel?"

"My ribs are slightly bruised and I am sure I will feel much worse in the morning, but otherwise I am in satisfactory condition and this brandy helps." He raised his glass.

"The nerve of those creeps. They must have been looking for trouble."

"Or perhaps someone put them up to it." Reginald tried to keep his eyes from straying to the hint of cleavage peeking from the loosened robe.

"Do you think someone paid those thugs to harass me in the bar so they could pick a fight with you?"

"Yes, or they may have been intercepted by someone who had been watching us, and paid to jump us sometime after we left the bar."

"Yeah, I would think they had enough after the thrashing you gave them with that stick."

"Oh yes, my old broken pool cue. How I miss it. Seriously though, someone could have been attempting to stop us from finding out where Gladys Fisk lives."

"And her husband, who just might be able to identify the one who sabotaged your airplane. Gladys and her husband both worked at the studio at the time of the accident. We definitely need to talk to Mrs. Fisk."

"The dear lady could be a wealth of information in regards to the goings on at Fairmont, besides helping us to find Mr. Fisk. We still do not have much to go on yet. One, we believe that the plane crash was sabotage. Two, we think that Brogan found a witness. Three, we are guessing Brogan's murder and the fire are connected," he counted off on his fingers.

"It all seems like nothing more than guesswork, doesn't it?" she said quietly.

"Yes, it does to me too, but we are not exactly professionals either. We are feeling around in the dark until we talk to more people."

"I know that we need to talk to this Fisk guy and Gladys, but who else can we talk to?"

"That fellow who lives above Mrs. Fisk mentioned that she is involved with a mechanic. "I wonder if it could be Don Denison?"

"Refresh my memory, who is Don Denison?" she asked.

"He is an aircraft mechanic who works for Fairmont. He was my mechanic until last year and may be able to tell us exactly how the plane was tampered with."

"You say he still works at the studio?"

"He works for the studio at their airfields. At least he did the last time I spoke to him, but that was several months ago."

"Well, we need to find him as soon as we can. Do you think he could be the one who rigged the plane? I mean, do you think he could be capable of doing something like that?"

"The police interviewed him after the crash, but he was not charged with any wrong doing. I don't see what his motive would be for intentionally causing my plane to crash and he certainly did not seem like a person who could do such a thing."

"But we just can't be sure, it's still possible that he could have some reason for sabotaging the biplane," she said.

"We will find Don and talk to him. If we ask enough questions, and get him talking about the accident, he may reveal something to us that was previously unknown."

"Yeah, like suppose he didn't sabotage the plane, I mean what if he made a mistake causing the wheel to come off and then he tried to cover it up."

68. T.E.Avery

"I don't know Alexis. You could be right, but it seems strange that the investigators never found any evidence that would incriminate Don."

"Then when you hired the detective, Don had to kill him to keep us from finding the truth. He set the fire to get rid of any evidence."

"Maybe, but let us go and look him up tomorrow. First we speak with Gladys and then with Don. Perhaps they will tell us something if we ask the right questions."

"Yeah, it sure doesn't seem like the police are trying very hard. Maybe we should talk to them too."

"Yes, we should ask them about the details of Brogan's death and about the fire if they will tell us anything," Reginald said.

"I think we need to talk to anyone who was at the crash scene, especially any investigators or police who were called."

"A good idea, if those people are still around. It has been a year and the trail grows colder every day. How is the brandy?"

"It's a little too strong for me, but it does help calm the nerves once you get it down and get over the initial burning sensation," she laughed.

"Sometimes I come down here at night to sip my brandy and think."

"What do you think about Reggie?"

He took some time to consider before answering.

"I think about Lillian quite a bit. The few months we spent together was the happiest time of my life. I also tend to remember some things that happened during the war. Mostly bad, but a few good times too. Sometimes we block out the really evil things that happened and only remember the people we cared about, or so it seems."

"Do you ever wonder about the future, your future I mean?"

"I have not considered my future for a very long time. I suppose things will be different for both of us if we find out what really happened with the plane crash."

"Yeah, I guess things will be kind of different if I don't have to spend all of my time wondering what really happened to my sister. It'll be good to know the truth and get on with our lives."

"You will get work as an actress, become a famous star, and forget all about this brief chapter in your life."

"Will we still see each other after it's over Reggie?" For some reason, this topic made Reginald uncomfortable and he abruptly changed the subject. "We should be thinking about getting some sleep if we are to get an early start tomorrow," he reminded her.

Reginald drained the last of his brandy, said goodnight, and went up to his room. Alexis remained in the leather chair thinking about her own future long after he had left.

Chapter 7.

The next morning they were sitting at the breakfast table eating a large meal prepared by Reginald's cook. They had both dressed in attire that would blend into almost any situation or neighborhood.

Reginald sported a double breasted pin striped suit made of light weight fabric. Alexis wore her most sensible light blue sleeveless dress. They did not want to draw unnecessary attention to themselves while going about their business as stand-in investigators.

As usual, Greta had prepared the food to perfection and she periodically came into the small dining room to check on their progress. "She gets on my nerves sometimes," Alexis said after the cook had returned to the kitchen. "I feel like she's spying on us."

Alexis had risen much earlier than Reginald, her sleep troubled by dreams involving being attacked by three smelly ogres. She shuddered to think what would have happened to them last night if Dominic had not come along when he did.

They were still sitting at the table when Greta returned, yet again, to clear away some of the dishes. "Is that a bruise on your cheek sir?" she asked unexpectedly.

"Why yes, it is Greta. Just a small one though. Nothing to be concerned about." Reginald replied.

"No sir, but you must be more careful. One can meet very rough people in this town and you never know what could happen."

This comment made Reginald and Alexis exchange questioning glances. How had she known that they had been visiting a rough area of the city? Greta noticed their surreptitious looks. "Anybody can clearly see it was a fist that made the bruise sir."

Greta pushed through the kitchen door shaking her head and muttering. "Not good. Not good."

"I think it would be a good idea for Dominic to remain here today when we go back into town," Reginald said.

"You mean to keep an eye on things around here?"

Murder By Plane 71.

Alexis stared at the kitchen door through which the Austrian cook had just exited.

"Yes, and I believe we will be much safer in broad daylight. No need for Dominic to tag along today."

"Okay, if you say so, but I can't stand the thought of going back into that neighborhood after last night's trouble."

"It is not absolutely necessary for you to accompany me Alexis. You can stay here if going back there frightens you."

"No. You can't get rid of me that easily Reginald. I need to be in on this too. I want to talk to that Fisk woman and find out what she knows. She could be the key to everything and besides, it is daytime. Like you said, we should be safer." Her tone did not sound convincing.

Later, she brought up the subject concerning the pistol he had retrieved from his desk before they left. "Why didn't you carry that thing last night? It might have come in handy," she said.

"It never really occurred to me we might be in that much danger last night, but now I'm not so sure. It is just a little insurance."

"Where did you get that cannon?"

"It is a Lebel M1892 revolver and I have had it since the war. It was standard issue for French officers and has been useful on several occasions."

"Do you mean during the war or after?"

"Why both, my girl," he said, almost cheerfully.

She looked at him askance to see if he was joking or not, but Reginald was focused on his driving now. What secrets did this man carry with him from the past, besides an odd skeleton key and a foreign military sidearm?" she thought. Alexis leaned forward, folded her arms tightly and kept these thoughts to herself as the big car raced down the hill into a valley of forgotten people.

72. T.E.Avery

Reginald parked the Duesenberg at the curb near the rundown tenement house, which had been the scene of their dangerous confrontation last night. They headed toward the front door only to find it was slightly ajar. Reginald stepped forward and immediately noticed that it had been forced. He knocked several times before finally pushing the wobbly door open. "I'll go in, you wait out here," he whispered.

"I'm not arguing," she said quietly. "Just be careful."

Reginald pulled out the old revolver, pointed it forward and advanced into the dark interior of the ramshackle abode, creeping slowly until his eyes adjusted.

When he could see again he was startled by what he now beheld. The small living room was a complete shambles. Several chairs and a table were overturned. Bottles and papers covered the floor. With a quick look behind the front door Reginald stepped further into the ravaged apartment. The tiny kitchen area resembled the wrecked front room. How pathetic, Reginald thought, as he looked around at the destruction of Gladys Fisk's few possessions. He peered at the bedroom door with a feeling of dread, not knowing what he might find.

Reginald walked slowly and carefully into the bedroom, trying not to disturb a possible crime scene. Perhaps a murder, he thought. Certainly the police would need to be called after his search was over.

Reginald let out a loud breath of relief that Gladys Fisk's body was not in the bedroom or bath. No other rooms remained in the diminutive space. There did not seem to be any closets at all.

Reginald picked his way carefully through the clutter and back to the entrance, putting away his pistol. He was glad to be out of the mess. Alexis waited anxiously at the side of the open door and he noticed relief register on her face when he appeared.

"Did you miss me?" He joked.

Murder By Plane 73.

"No, but I thought the cops would come any minute and arrest us. What did you find in there?" she asked, with some trepidation apparent in her tone.

"Not much really. Mrs. Fisk is obviously not at home, but someone has completely destroyed her place, as if they were searching for something."

"What now?" she asked.

"I suppose we must contact the police and let them know what has occurred here, if someone has not done so already. We could go upstairs and talk to her neighbor and ask him to call the authorities. He may even know what happened in Mrs. Fisk's apartment."

"I hope he's in a better mood this time," she said.

"He may not even be home at this time of day."

They took the rickety stairs to the second floor landing and once again Reginald pounded on the door until it was answered by the ill-tempered man. He was wearing the same clothes from the evening before and held an unfiltered cigarette loosely from thin, nicotine stained, lips.

"Yeah? Oh, you again?"

"What happened downstairs?" Reginald asked.

"How should I know?"

"Well, we thought since you live right above her...."

"Look, I don't know nothin about nothin. I mind my own business, see."

"Were the police here?"

"Yeah, they came."

"Is Mrs. Fisk all right?"

"Yeah, she's okay," the bald man said.

He's being tightlipped about something, Reginald thought.

"Do you know where she is?"

"Like I said. I mind my own business."

"We need to speak with her. It could be a matter of great urgency," Alexis said.

"Urgent for you maybe. Not me. Now beat it."

This time Reginald stepped forward, grabbed a

74. T.E.Avery

handful of dirty undershirt, practically lifting the scruffy man off of his feet. "Look Mr., the lady said it was important and you had better tell us what you know." Reginald let go and the man retreated a step back, his face a mask of fear. He started to talk very rapidly.

"I don't want no trouble, see. I heard a bunch a noise comin from downstairs. It woke me from a sound sleep. Later on, I was woke up by Gladys beatin on my door. She said somebody trashed her place. She used my phone to call the cops and her sister."

"Did you talk to the police?" Reginald asked.

"Uh, yeah. They come up here to ask a bunch a questions just like you. I told em the same as I'm telling you. I don't know who done it."

"You didn't go to the window to see what was causing the disturbance?" Alexis asked.

"Well, yeah. I did, but it was kinda dark out. I couldn't see nothin."

"What did Mrs. Fisk tell you?" Reginald prodded.

"She was real scared. She couldn't hardly even talk on account a bein scared so I gives her a shot a whiskey to calm her nerves down, see. Like I said, she calls the cops and then her sister. She waited here till they came. That's all I know," he shrugged.

"Do you know where her sister lives?" Reginald asked.

"Nope."

"The police could, at least, have secured her front door," Alexis said.

"Are you kiddin lady? Those cops won't even be back. I'll bet they never even filed a report. They don't care about us. That woman lost everythin she owned when that guy broke in and trashed her place."

"I thought you said you didn't see anyone,"Alexis said.

"I forgot, see,"He glanced nervously at Reginald. "I remember now, I seen a man leavin the place and goin down the street. I heard a car start up and go off down the road. And that's all I remember, I swear, see."

"I see," mocked Reginald. "All right then, thanks. Here is something for your trouble." Reginald handed him a five.

"Thanks, Mr. St. John." He snatched the bill and slammed the door.

Reginald turned to Alexis with a deadpan expression straight out of the silent comedies.

"And you thought people didn't know you." She laughed, but her expression turned serious. "Who do you think broke into her apartment Reggie?"

They walked downstairs to Gladys's flat.

"Perhaps someone was trying to find information," he replied.

"Maybe it was the thugs we had trouble with last night? They would be capable of doing something like this."

"That could be, but our friend upstairs said he saw only one man and he heard a car pull away. That does not sound like those losers from last night."

"Yeah, I don't think those bums even own a car, so who was it?"

"I wonder if it could have been the killer looking for any information on Mr. Fisk's whereabouts?"

"Yeah, it's a rough neighborhood, but it would still be quite a coincidence if this happened just before we came along searching for information."

"I believe there must be some connection between what happened here and our looking for the witness," Reginald stated.

"Now we have to find out where Gladys Fisk went before we can find Mr. Fisk," Alexis said. "This is really getting frustrating Reggie. We aren't making any progress at all."

"The man upstairs said the police won't be back. Why don't we go in and search for her sister's address?" Reginald asked. "It must be written down somewhere."

"Yeah, and maybe we could talk to the old woman across the street. She might have seen something this morning that the guy upstairs didn't."

"An excellent idea, I just hope I haven't run out of five dollar bills."

They decided to go across the street first. Reginald knocked on the dilapidated entrance and after several long minutes it opened a crack. "Yeah?" the voice croaked.

"Hello again. We would like to ask you some questions please."

"What's the trouble?"

"We were just wondering if you had seen anything strange going on across the street?"

"You mean that fight that happened last night?"

"No, we know all about that," Reginald glanced at Alexis. "We were thinking about early this morning."

"Do you mean when the police were over there?"

"Well, before that actually. Did you notice anyone entering or leaving the ground floor apartment?"

"I'm an old woman you know, I don't stay up to all hours spying on my neighbors. I try to mind my own affairs."

Reginald held up a five. "Does this help to refresh your memory?"

The old woman took the note without missing a beat. "I did see a man leaving sometime around two o'clock this morning."

"My, you do have an accurate memory for a woman your age. Good reflexes too. Can you describe him to us?"

"My eyes aren't very good. I'm old you know. I couldn't make out his face, but he wasn't very tall and he was all dressed in dark clothes."

"The man who lives in the upstairs apartment said he walked down the street to a car and drove away. Did you see him go in that direction?"

"Yeah, but you know what? He weren't walking

very fast for somebody that done something wrong."

"Did you see or hear anything else?" Alexis asked.

"Not until that poor woman came home from work and found her place broke into. I could hear her screaming bloody murder. And I'm old, you know."

"Yes, I know."

"Well, you don't have to be rude." She abruptly slammed the door in his face, almost hitting his nose.

"Nice going again Sherlock." Alexis kicked his shin.

"Ouch, hey. Why did you do that?" He pinched the end of her small nose.

"Hey. Let go Reggie. Well, we won't be getting anymore information out of her now."

"You started it." He shook his finger in her face. "Besides, we probably got all of the information we could anyway and I'm out of fives."

They went back to Gladys's apartment to begin the tedious search for her sister's address.

"This is like looking for a needle in a haystack Reggie. We don't even know her sister's name."

The two had better luck in the light of day than the previous searcher.

"Here is a pile of envelopes scattered near the wall," Reginald said.

"It looks mostly like bills to me." Alexis looked over his shoulder. "What's that one?"

"Aha, this could be something. It is the address of a woman who does not live far away from here. It could be her sister."

"I hope she's at home. This could be an exercise in futility Reggie. What if she doesn't even know where Mr. Fisk is?"

"She must know something or the killer would not have targeted her. Now let's get going before someone calls the police." Reginald rubbed his leg. "And my shin still hurts."

"Sorry," she said without much feeling.

"I'll bet you are," he said.

78. T.E.Avery

"Do you really think it was the murderer that broke into her home?" she asked.

"Who else, my girl? What could Gladys Fisk possibly own that anyone would want?"

"He must be after the whereabouts of Mr. Fisk, and that means ...."

"That Mr. Fisk can positively identify him as the saboteur and murderer," Reginald said.

"Exactly, my boy." She held up an index finger in exaggerated triumph.

"I still find you to be greatly annoying at times, Kansas," he said.

Alexis ignored the taunt. "Do you think Gladys will talk to us?"

"I certainly hope so, because she may be our only way to solve this mess."

"Yeah, she's beginning to remind me of that skeleton key of yours. She is the only way to unlock this case," she said.

"Let's just hope we can get the information from her before she really becomes a skeleton."

"Now that is creepy," she complained.

They drove slowly through the streets of Los Angeles where row upon row of ramshackle houses stood in silent testimony to the depressed economy in this area of the city. They did not notice a small black car as it pulled away from the curb and began to follow them.

"Why did you have to get so rough with that old guy in the upstairs apartment Reggie?"

He shrugged. "I have found that, at certain times, fear is a good motivation. Especially when it is something as important as this."

"I suppose you learned that during the war?" she asked.

"Yes, mostly during the war, but also at other times in my life."

"You can be so complicated at times, Mr. Reginald St. John," she said with obvious frustration.

Murder By Plane 79.

"Why do you say that, Kansas?"

"At times you seem so kind, polite and mild mannered, but at other times you are ...."

"...Cold, brutal, barbaric?" he finished.

"All of the above," she said.

"Well, I think everyone has a good side and a bad side. Am I correct?"

"I guess you might have a point, but it just took me by surprise in your case."

"You mean you did not see me as a fighter?"

"Not lately anyway. You seemed to be so spiritless and despondent."

"Perhaps you bring out the savage beast in me, my girl."

Reginald turned suddenly down a side street, as if he knew the area.

"Have you been here before Reggie?"

"Yes, a few times. This neighborhood is not nearly as decrepit as where Gladys lives."

"So you know where her sister lives?" she asked.

"No, I know someone else who lives here and I want to make a quick call. It will only take a few minutes."

He found the small neat house that he was looking for and pulled up to the curb.

"Who do you know in this neighborhood Reggie?"

"This is where Grace Robinson, my cook, lives. I want to see how she is doing and I would like you to meet her. I hope that you don't mind."

The door was answered by an elderly black man with gray hair and mustache. His face registered surprise, followed quickly by a wide smile.

"Mr. St. John. It's good of you to stop by. Please come in," he said.

"We can only stay a few minutes Arthur. We are in the neighborhood and I wanted to check in on Grace. How is she?"

"She's right in here sir. You can ask her yourself," Arthur said with another grin.

Chapter 8.

"Hello Grace." Reginald took her hand in his. "How is your leg?"

She was a small pleasant looking black woman who looked to be in her mid fifties, but was actually ten years older. She sat in a comfortable chair near the radio. Her hands had been busily knitting something that now rested on her lap along with a calico cat. "I'm doing much better now, thank you. It's so good to see you Mr. Reginald. I wanted to thank you for everything you've done for us." Tears welled in her eyes.

"It was the least I could do for the best cook in Los Angeles. This is Alexis Moxley. Alexis, this is Grace Robinson," Reginald said.

Reginald inquired politely about her condition and when he could expect her back in his kitchen. He also asked details about the car wreck that had injured her leg. She explained that she had been driving her old Model T to work when a larger automobile shot out of an alley, broadsided her, and drove away. She related she was unaware of what had occurred until a witness came forward and told the police what happened. After a short, but warm and friendly conversation, they said their goodbyes to Grace and Arthur.

"What wonderful people," Alexis said after they were seated in the car again. "I bet you are looking forward to her return and getting rid of that Greta woman."

"Yes, to both statements, my girl."

"You know, it almost seems that Grace's accident was a set-up."

"How do you mean?" he asked.

"Well, it seems kind of fishy to me. The way she described that car coming out of the alley and then driving away like that," she said.

"I tend to believe it was nothing more than a hit and run accident. Those things happen all the time," he said with a wave of his hand. "Whoever hit Grace was simply someone trying to avoid responsibility."

"I suppose you could be right, but it sure

Murder By Plane 81.

sounds suspicious to me," she said. "By the way," she continued, "What was it you did for Grace and her husband after the accident?"

"Nothing really," Reginald sounded embarrassed, "I just helped them out a little with money and another car. Hers was totally destroyed. What else could I do?"

They continued down the main avenue until they came to the address matching the one on the envelope.

"I hope the address is Gladys sister's and we haven't come here for nothing."

"I suppose that is why it takes so much patience to be a detective, my girl."

"What would you know about being a detective?"

"Well, I did play a detective in several pictures. You remember those films I made several years ago don't you?"

"I think those were before my time. And that doesn't make you an expert detective either," she said.

"It is certainly more experience than you can lay claim to, Kansas."

"Stop calling me Kansas," she said a little too loudly.

"My my, are we being testy today?" He parked the car by the curb.

"I'm just nervous about meeting Gladys Fisk. She can help us solve this mystery, but what if she doesn't? Do you have enough money on you to bribe her into talking?"

"Alright stop." He moved closer to her, took her small hand, rubbed it gently and looked into her eyes. "Take a deep breath Alexis and we will go over some questions we can ask Mrs. Fisk after we make some polite conversation to set her at ease,"

His perfect voice had become even smoother and Alexis blinked several times. She realized no words were coming out of her mouth. She felt her muscles relaxing.

"Have you thought of anything to ask Mrs. Fisk?"

82. T.E.Avery

"Yes," she said softly. "I want to ask her where her no good lousy ex-husband is."

"Yes, well, perhaps a little more delicate than that, my girl. Anything else?"

"We could ask her about the break-in at her apartment. Does she suspect anyone?"

"Yes, and also her job at the studio," he said.

"Her relationship with that mechanic guy at the studio. Don something," she said.

"But mainly we must ask her if she knows where her ex-husband can be found. Do you feel calmer now?" he asked.

"Yeah, I do. How did you do that?"

"What did I do now? You are so very exasperating sometimes," he muttered.

The two actors appeared out of place, in this section of town, as they exited the Duesenberg. They were again being watched from a car parked further down the street.

"I hope she's home, I hope she's home, I hope she's home," Alexis chanted the mantra to herself as they ascended the front steps of the house. Reginald looked at her as if he were considering her sanity.

"I think it would be best if you allow me to question Mrs. Fisk," he said.

"Why, do you think I can't handle myself around people?"

"I think I am a little more experienced in these matters than you are," Reginald added.

"In what matters? You're an actor for gosh sakes," Alexis said.

"You seem to be out of sorts today. Perhaps we will have lunch after we are finished here," he said.

"Oh, so now I'm a kid who needs my dinner to quiet me down?" Her hands were on her hips. "I suppose you think I need a nap too?"

"Well, now that you mention it," he smirked.

"Ooh, I oughta kick you."

"We must have a long discussion concerning your kicking habit."

"Are you going to knock?" she asked, hand on hip.

The door was answered, after a few knocks, by a matronly woman who appeared to be in her late fifties. She wore a pink flowered cotton dress and hair pinned at the back of her head into a bun, adding years to her face. Thick spectacles partially hid her eyes.

"Yes?" she asked timidly.

"We are looking for a Mrs. Gladys Fisk," Reginald said in his most disarming tone.

"And who are you sir?" He could see recognition on her face.

"I am Reginald St. John and this is Alexis Moxley. Are you Mrs. Fisk?"

"No, I'm her sister," she blushed. "She's sleeping and can't be disturbed. I'll tell her you want to see her and she can call you back later Mr. St. John."

"We know what happened at her home last night," Reginald stated without preamble.

"You know about the break in? Is that why you came to see her? I don't understand," she asked, sounding confused.

"We went to her apartment to talk to her about another matter and the door was unsecured. We thought something had happened to Mrs. Fisk so we looked in and saw the damage. It is a terrible tragedy and I'm very sorry."

"Yes, she was so devastated by it all," she said.

"May we please come in for just a few minutes?" Reginald said in his most charming voice.

"Maybe for a few minutes," she hesitated. "But you still can't talk to my sister."

The cluttered living room smelled of stale cigarettes, cooking odors and cats; radio blaring out the remainder of a newscast. The announcer was saying something about Germany's new chancellor and his latest speech.

"Thank you, you are very kind. You have not

introduced yourself yet," Reginald said in a pleasant voice.

"I'm Lois. Lois Sneed. I've never met a real movie star before," she said self consciously. "Won't you sit down? And please don't mind the mess. I've been taking care of my sister all day."

Reginald expected her to curtsy at any minute, as if he and Alexis were royalty, and not an out of work actress and a Hollywood has-been. "Thank you Mrs. Sneed," he said.

"Can I get you two something to drink? I have tea or something stronger if you like."

"No thank you Mrs. Sneed," Reginald said.

"No thanks," Alexis chimed.

"You can call me Lois," she said. Lois sat in a tattered, overstuffed chair.

"We need to locate Mr. Fisk to ask him some questions. There are some other things we need to discuss with Mrs. Fisk," Reginald continued in his velvety smooth voice.

"Why would anyone want to talk to Joe Fisk?" Lois asked.

"We believe he can provide us with important information we are seeking," Reginald replied.

"Oh, important huh?" Lois said quietly as if in a hypnotic state.

"Yes, its very important and we need to speak with your sister as soon as possible Lois, so can you please wake her and we will have a few words with her."

Reginald spoke in a soft, calm voice and Alexis felt herself relaxing. The room was warm and the old cushion very soft. Reginald looked over at Alexis and gave her a nudge with his elbow. She jerked and sat up straight on the sofa.

"I'll see if she can talk to you Mr. St. John." Lois stood woodenly and went through a door, into what they assumed to be a bedroom.

"What are you doing?" Alexis whispered.

Murder By Plane 85.

"I told you that you needed a nap young lady. I thought you were going to doze off any second," he snickered quietly.

"Shut up. Are you some kind of hypnotist or something?" Alexis asked crossly.

"I will explain later, now is not a good time."

"Yes, you'd better explain. At least we finally found Gladys Fisk."

Lois came back into the room followed by a woman who looked to be several years younger than her sister. It was clear Gladys Fisk had been attractive at one time, but apparent, by her ruddy complexion, she drank too much. The years, and abuse, had not been kind to her. She appeared to be under sedation. Lois helped her out of the bedroom and to a chair.

"Hello Mrs. Fisk. How are you?" Reginald began.

"Who are you?" Gladys asked through bleary eyes.

"I told you dear," Lois said. "This is Reginald St. John, you know, the movie star."

"Oh, okay," Gladys slurred.

"We need to ask you a few simple questions Mrs. Fisk."

"About what?" she asked.

"Do you know the whereabouts of Joe Fisk?"

"You mean the derelict that I kicked out? I ain't seen him for awhile."

"Yes, but do you know where we might locate him?" Reginald asked.

"How should I know where that bum is? I tell ya I ain't seen him in over a year."

"We have reason to believe you may know how to find him," Reginald said.

"Oh, is that so Mr. Movie star?" she burst into sobs. "Well, you don't know what I been through lately." Her sister put a consoling arm around her.

"We know about your apartment Mrs. Fisk. I am very sorry," he said with sympathy.

"Do you know who might have done such a thing?" Alexis asked.

"No, that's just it," Gladys dabbed her eyes with a handkerchief provided by Lois. "I got no enemies and I don't have anything that anyone would want anyhow."

"Was anything taken from the apartment?" Reginald asked.

"Nothing that I could see. It was such a mess I couldn't tell anyway, but I don't think anything was stolen," Gladys shook her head and looked up toward the ceiling. "Why me?"

"I must be perfectly honest with both of you ladies," Reginald began. "The detective I hired to locate your ex-husband was killed. That is why we decided to take it on ourselves to find out what we need to know. We believe someone murdered the private investigator to prevent him from finding out where Joe Fisk can be found. This murderer may be the same one who broke into your place."

"But why my sister's apartment?" Lois asked.

"The killer desperately wants to find Joe Fisk and he broke into her home in order to find information that would lead him to Mr. Fisk," Reginald answered.

"Mr. Fisk? Ha. What does Joe have that anybody would possibly want?" Gladys asked.

"Joe Fisk was a security guard at Fairmont Studios wasn't he?" Reginald asked.

"Only for a little while and that was almost a year ago. That bum can't hold onto a job," Gladys said.

"Apparently he must have witnessed something that incriminates someone, and that someone wants to shut him up for good," Reginald said.

"You mean someone wants to kill Joe?" Lois asked.

"We think so and we are trying to find him before the killer does," he said.

"What did he witness?" Gladys asked.

"A murder or at least someone deliberately causing an accident that resulted in a death," Reginald said.

Murder By Plane 87.

"Can you tell us anything about where Mr. Fisk can be found?"

"Hey, I just remembered something. There was a man asking me the same thing a few days ago," Gladys said. "At least I think it was a few days ago, I'm not so sure."

"That may have been the detective I hired, Frank Brogan," Reginald said.

"And somebody killed him?" Gladys asked.

"Yes and his killer is trying to find your ex-husband, Mrs. Fisk," Reginald reminded.

"Yeah, I remember that guy at the bar. He was real nice to me, it's a shame he got murdered like that." Gladys and Lois both shook their heads sadly.

"Do you have any idea where we might find Joe Fisk?" Reginald asked.

"Ah, well, he probably stays under a bridge somewhere, but I know where he likes to hang out and shoot pool," Gladys slurred.

"Can you give us directions to this place Mrs. Fisk?"

"Yeah, my sister can write it down for you. I'm not feeling too good right now."

"I understand madam," Reginald said.

"Just call me Gladys," she smiled.

"Do you presently work at Fairmont Studios Gladys?"

"Yeah, I work at the studios. Why?" She asked in an irritated voice.

"How long have you been employed there Gladys?"

"Too long. Lois, I need another drink to clear my head. Be a dear and pour me a small glass of whiskey," Gladys said.

"Do you think you should Gladys?" Lois asked.

"Just a small one to get the cobwebs out hon," Gladys whined.

"Well, okay deary." Lois went into the kitchen for the liquor.

"Are you acquainted with a mechanic named Don Denison, Gladys?" Reginald asked.

"I know Don," Gladys said.

"Does he still work at the studio?"

"Yeah, he still works there," she said.

Lois came back into the room with the drink and handed it to Gladys, who immediately took a large quaff. "Thanks dear." She downed the entire drink. "Don't you folks want one?"

"No thank you Gladys. How well do you know Don Denison?"

"We get together for a drink now and then, just having some fun," she said.

"Has he ever told you anything about an airplane crash that happened last year?"

"No, like I said, we get together to have fun. We don't talk about serious stuff too much," she said.

"Do you remember the crash Gladys? The airplane accident last year?" he repeated.

"Yeah, hey, that was you. I remember it now. Wow, so you are asking around about it now?"

"Yes, we have reason to believe that it was not an accident Gladys," he said.

"You mean you think someone might have done something to cause the plane to crash?" Lois asked.

"We believe so Mrs. Sneed," Reginald replied.

"Oh my, and you think the killer is still around?" Lois hugged herself.

"Yes, we want to get to Joe Fisk before the killer," Alexis said.

"I'll write down those directions for you Mr. St. John," Lois said.

"Did Don Denison tell you anything about the accident Gladys?" he asked again.

"I think he did mention something about missing tools, but you should probably ask him yourself," Gladys said.

"Did he feel responsible because he was the last one to work on the plane?" Alexis asked.

"I don't know, ask him," Gladys said.

"What about your ex-husband?" Reginald asked.

"What about him? He's a bum," she said.

"You told Frank Brogan your husband witnessed something Gladys," Reginald said.

"Yeah, I think he saw somebody sneaking around," she said.

"Tell me exactly what he told you he saw," he said.

"I need another drink before I can remember," she said quietly.

Gladys waited for her sister to pour another whiskey before she continued.

"He came home from work that night and said he'd seen a man walking around the hanger. Joe called out to the guy and ran over to the hanger, but the man had gone. He heard a car driving off. That's all he told me," she said.

"Did he come forward and report this to the police, after the accident, the next day?" Reginald asked.

"He might have if he'd still been around. He got plastered that night and started slapping me around. I told him to get out and never come back. It's been nearly a year now."

"You haven't heard from him since?" Alexis asked.

"I saw the jerk standing on a corner beggin for change a couple months ago."

"Did he specify that he might have recognized the intruder?" Reginald asked.

"He might have said that he recognized the guy, I don't know," Gladys replied.

"What else can you tell us about Joe Fisk?"

"He's a bum."

"Besides that fact."

"He has a daughter from another marriage. He talked about her all the time, drove me crazy with it."

"That is not so unusual though. Many fathers are

proud of their children Mrs. Fisk," Reginald said.

"Well he was obsessed about his precious little girl. He drove me nuts talking about her all the time. Clara, Clara, Clara. That's all I heard. The night I kicked him out he was going on about her. I got sick of hearing about it and I told him so. He raised his hand to me and I kicked the bum out."

"What did you say his daughter's name was Gladys?" Reginald asked.

"Clara Fisk."

"Do you know her well?"

"Are you kiddin? That dame thought she was too good for the likes of us."

Gladys was on her third whiskey and it was apparent in her speech.

"Did his daughter live nearby?" Alexis asked.

"Well, yeah honey, she was a movie star and that's all I ever heard him talk about. Clara this and Clara that. I think he was just after her money if you ask me, cause he never wanted anything to do with his daughter until she got famous."

"Exactly who is his daughter? Perhaps I know her," Reginald asked.

"Well, you should know her Mr. St. John; she's Claire Cauldwell, the actress."

"Claire Cauldwell is his daughter?" Reginald asked in astonishment. He looked over at Alexis, who also had a surprised expression on her face.

"That's right, Claire Cauldwell, and she's all I ever heard him talk about. Clara, Clara, Clara," Gladys said.

"Are you sure we are talking about The Claire Cauldwell, silent screen star?"

"I'm sure all right, that's how Joe got his job at the studio, her pulling the right strings so her old man could get work. But he never could hold down a job, cause he's a ...."

"A bum, I know, but what happened to Claire?" Reginald asked.

"It's sad really. Her career took a dive when the talkies come out. You probably know all this anyway; she went kind of crazy, got into booze and drugs. Last I heard she was put in the state asylum. What comes around goes around, that's what I always say," She lifted her glass in a salute.

"That is so sad," Alexis said.

"Did you say it was a State institution?" Reginald asked.

"Yeah, the bum would go see her once in a while, I waited in the lobby," Gladys said.

"I'll write the address down for you Mr. St. John," Lois said.

"Thank you," Reginald said absently. "You have both been most helpful; please tell me if there is ever anything I can do for you."

"Well, maybe you could help me out just a little, I was hit pretty hard last night, with my place being tore up and all," Gladys slurred.

"Gladys please. Show some respect, my goodness," Lois reddened.

"Respect can't replace my stuff that I lost," Gladys said.

Reginald accepted the directions from Lois and handed her two fifty dollar bills to help her sister. He also warned them both about admitting anyone else into their house until the killer was found.

"You should remain here with your sister Mrs. Fisk, I think it will be safer for you," he said. Reginald and Alexis stepped out into the afternoon sun, glad to be out of the stuffy interior. The front porch was a pleasant change after the depressing interview.

"I still can't believe what she said about Claire Cauldwell, Reggie," Alexis said.

"I cannot believe it either. I knew Claire had been having problems when sound was introduced to pictures, but I never thought for a minute she had taken it so hard."

"So the silent screen darling of the world is the daughter of a derelict," Alexis stated.

"The poor girl must have wanted to make it big in Hollywood just to get out of poverty."

"She would have if it had not been for the talkies. She was very successful in the silent films, but lacked the voice training to make it in sound pictures."

"But Lillian did," Alexis said.

"Yes, there was never anyone like your sister. She was born to be an actress," Reginald said.

"You made it into the talkies," she said as they walked to the car.

"I had the stage training from my youth," he stated.

"Do you think Joe Fisk might have sabotaged the plane?" Alexis asked.

"I suppose it could be possible, but what would his motive be and why would he tell his wife about an intruder at the hanger that night?"

"Gladys said he was obsessed with his daughter, maybe he wanted to get revenge for her. The failure of her career must have devastated them both," she said.

"He loved his daughter for her wealth and fame according to Gladys," Reginald said.

"It's pretty plain to see Gladys is a big lush. She could be making all of this up," Alexis said as Reginald opened her door.

"It's good to know someone out there drinks more than I do," he said.

"What's the next move Houdini?" she asked. Reginald ignored the taunt. "I think we should head home first and later we will see about finding Mr. Fisk."

"Why home?" she asked. He thought she looked disappointed.

"I want to have lunch at home and I have something to ask Dominic," he stated.

"Shouldn't we try to find Joe Fisk as soon as possible Reggie?"

Murder By Plane 93.

"Joe Fisk will have to wait another hour or two, I'm starving," he said.

Reginald punched the accelerator pedal and they sped toward the Pacific coast and his house by the sea.

"Okay, now let's talk about your mysterious powers Mr. St. John," Alexis said as they traveled home.

"Powers? I don't know what you mean," he said.

"You know perfectly well what I'm talking about Reggie. What happened back there when you were speaking to Lois? You hypnotized that woman, didn't you?"

"No, I did not hypnotize her. I was only trying to get her to relax a little so that she would cooperate with us."

"Well, I would definitely say you got her to cooperate. She would have taken her clothes off if you had asked her to."

"Oh please, I did not have, that much, control over her Alexis," he said.

"So, you admit it. You had some sort of control. What are you hiding?"

"Hiding? I do not have anything to hide," Reginald said.

"You have some deep dark secret, don't you?"

"No, I don't," he said.

"Yes, you do," she said.

"No."

"Yes."

"Oh, all right then, I have practiced voice training since I was a child and have utilized this ah ... talent at certain times throughout my life. Now are you happy?"

"You can hypnotize people and control them. I knew you could.

"No."

"Yes."

"Oh, if you want to call it that. I suppose I can control some people, especially those who do not have strong willpower."

"You even used your powers to calm me before we went into the house to meet with Gladys. Wow, I am impressed," she said with genuine excitement.

"Powers? I would not exactly phrase it in those terms."

"Have you ever used your ah... power to seduce a woman?"

"Perhaps," he said jokingly.

"Did you use them on Lillian?"

"Lillian and I romanced each other, my girl. What we possessed was special to both of us."

"What about Claire Cauldwell?"

"What about her?" he asked.

"Did you have a relationship with her before you met my sister?"

"No. There was an initial attraction in the beginning, but nothing ever came of it."

"Why not?" she asked.

"How can I put this without sounding conceited? Claire was a woman of very loose morals and unstable emotions. I could never be attracted to someone like that."

"Oh, now I understand. She slept with a lot of men," she said with a nod.

"Claire would do whatever it took to get what she wanted," he said.

"What about Bruno Von Heller? Do you think she slept with him?"

"I would not be surprised. She had no discernment."

"Do you think she could be capable of murder?" Alexis asked.

"I don't know, anything is possible I suppose."

Chapter 9.

Dominic met them in the driveway, swaggering to the car as it pulled in. "Hi boss, everythin okay?"

"Yes Dominic, we came by to have lunch at home. Will you tell Greta to prepare something eatable for us please," Reginald instructed.

"She not here, she fly the coop." Dominic gestured.

"What are you talking about man?"

"I think Dom is telling us that your cook has left you," Alexis said.

"That's right boss, she leave about a hour ago."

"Did she take a cab?"

"No, a black car," Dominic said.

"Did you see who was at the wheel of the black car Dominic?"

"I only seen them a little bit boss, you know, si-ways."

"Profile?" Alexis asked.

"Yeah, I guess that's it." The big Sicilian shrugged.

"Did Greta say anything to you before she left? Could it have been an emergency?"

"No boss, I been watchin her like a eagle all morning, just like you say to do. She don't say a word," Dominic said.

"Could Greta have met somebody for lunch or gone to an appointment?" Alexis asked.

"She should not have gone without telling someone or leaving a note at least," Reginald said. "And she always took a cab before."

"She fly the coop," Dominic said with a sweep of his massive arm.

"Yes, that is apparent," Reginald said.

"Do you think it was something we said to her Reggie? Remember what we were talking about this morning. She knew we had been in a rough section of town last night. How is that possible?" Alexis asked.

"Yes, and she seemed extremely uncomfortable when she thought we had noticed her comment," Reginald stated.

96. T.E.Avery

"What if she wasn't really who she said she was and …," Alexis began.

"And she thought we were on to her. Dominic said he observed her all day. She got spooked and …."

"She fly the coop," Alexis and Dominic said in unison. Reginald arched an eyebrow.

"She became frightened and gave up her subterfuge. I wonder who she really is and whom she might be working for?" Reginald speculated.

"Now who gonna do the cookin around here boss?" Dominic asked.

"I think I can handle that if you will allow me Reggie. I hope you don't mind Midwest cooking," Alexis said.

"You gonna be the cook Miss Moxley?" Dominic pointed.

"Well, why not? We have to eat don't we?" she asked.

"Your sister would not have been caught dead in the kitchen. Oh, sorry, I didn't mean for it to come out that way," Reginald said.

Alexis prepared a cold cut lunch for the three of them, but Dominic decided to take his to the garage, thanking her and making the excuse he had work to do. Reginald knew the Italian was embarrassed to be served by the young actress and it would take some time for him to get used to the idea.

Alexis wasn't like her sister at all. There was a remarkable resemblance, yet Alexis behaved older than her years, whereas Lillian often seemed immature in many ways. There were definite characteristics of both women he found, or had found, in Lillian's case, very exasperating. Lillian would take hours to ready herself to go somewhere, but Alexis could be set to go in minutes. Lillian envisioned herself as a great lady and would hardly speak to the servants.

Alexis prepared lunch for Dominic, much to his chagrin. Reginald watched her as she finished arranging

Murder By Plane 97.
the sandwiches on the plates and brought them to the table. Yes, this could take a little getting used to. "Now that looks delicious. Thank you, my girl."

"It's just a sandwich, no big deal," she said

Reginald took a bite. "It is really very tasty."

"How will you find out about Greta? Where she went, I mean."

"I am not certain yet. Perhaps I could ask Max to look into it for me. He has contacts that may be able to trace her," he said. "And we will be busy the rest of the day."

"Where do you want to go after we finish lunch?" she asked.

"We should try to locate Joe Fisk first," Reginald said.

"Yeah, that should be our top priority. What about after that?"

"I would like to visit Claire in the asylum," he said quietly.

"Why?" she asked.

"I want to ask her some questions about her whereabouts the night before the accident, and I must see for myself if she is really in that place," he said.

"It is hard to imagine isn't it?" she asked before taking a huge bite.

"Hard to imagine she is staying in an asylum or someone could be driven to madness by desperation?" he asked.

"Both, I suppose. What about that mechanic guy, should we try to see him today?"

"Don Denison? I think we should have a few words with him. He is supposedly the last one to work on the Nieuport before the crash occurred. I want to know his movements that night as well."

"Gladys said he usually works late at the hanger," Alexis said.

"Works or drinks?"

"Maybe he was drinking the night he was working on

the plane and he left something off. A mistake causing an accident," she said.

"It could be, but the police cleared him and I think you are forgetting about the things that have happened thus far," he said.

"Yeah, like the fire, Brogan's death and Gladys's apartment," she said.

"Those thugs that attacked us too," He reminded. "This person has been operating strictly behind the scenes, I wonder if he could be flushed out?"

"That sounds like a script in one of your films Mr. St. John," Alexis said.

"It was used in more than one detective picture, my girl," he said.

The Stockton State Mental Hospital was an imposing brick and stucco structure. Constructed in 1853 on 100 acres of land, donated by Captain Weber to handle the large numbers of psychiatric patients created by the gold rush. It was the first public mental hospital in California.

Reginald and Alexis examined the giant edifice as the Duesenberg pulled up to the front walkway. Dominic exited the car to open the rear door for the pair, but he remained behind as they walked toward the entrance. Reginald could feel only sadness at the thought of Claire Cauldwell and her declining career. She had started out so promising, he thought, only to end up in a depressing place like this.

Reginald's mind was still occupied with these dreary thoughts when they entered the massive front doors. They were approached by an orderly in the standard white coat, which seemed too snug for his portly frame.

"How may I help you?" the overweight man asked.

"We need to speak with one of your patients on a most urgent personal matter," Reginald said.

"May I ask who it is you want to see?"

"Miss Claire Cauldwell," Reginald said.

Murder By Plane 99.

"Do you have an appointment sir?"

"No, but we must talk to Miss Cauldwell, it is very important."

"Please wait here. I'll get the superintendent," the man said.

He left them standing in the large bare foyer with a lone desk and chair. After what seemed to them an eternity of waiting in the tomb-like room, he returned with a smaller man dressed in a brown suit. The smaller man had features that Reginald thought resembled a rodent with thick spectacles.

"Hello, I am Dr. Shrewsberry. How may I help you?" The small man asked with a smile that gave them chills.

"Dr. Shrewsberry, it is of the utmost urgency that we speak to Claire Cauldwell," Reginald said.

"Claire Cauldwell?"

"Yes Doctor, it is very important. We must see her now," Reginald said.

"I am sorry sir, but Claire is not a patient at this hospital," the miniscule man said with yet another disturbing smile.

"Oh, we were told she was here by a reliable source, Doctor," Reginald said.

"Miss Cauldwell was with us until about three weeks ago Mr. St. John."

Reginald was not surprised the psychiatrist knew him. "Did she escape?"

"No, no," The tiny man chuckled. "This is not a prison Mr. St. John; she was not here against her will. Miss Cauldwell was free to leave at any time."

"How long had she been a patient doctor?" Alexis asked.

"Miss Cauldwell was in and out for over two years. She suffered from several different mental disorders exacerbated by alcohol and drug use. I am really not at liberty to discuss this with anyone. I have said too much already."

"Do you know where she is now?" Reginald asked.

"No sir. We have many patients here and it is impossible to keep track of them all once they are released."

"Can you at least give us her address?" Alexis asked.

"I can provide you with her last known address, but you must tell me the reason you want to locate her."

"She may be dangerous to herself and others," Reginald said. "I know this sounds crazy...."

"We do not use that word around here sir." The doctor looked from side to side.

"We believe Claire Cauldwell may know something concerning an accident that occurred about a year ago," Reginald continued. "It involved the death of my fiancée."

"My sister," Alexis added.

"Very well, if it is an emergency, but you must realize Claire often moved from place to place and she may not be at this address."

"Did her father ever come to visit her doctor?" Alexis asked.

"Yes, he visited Claire on several occasions," the doctor said.

"Do you have his address?" Reginald asked.

"I will have someone look up the addresses we have on file for Miss Cauldwell."

"Thank you Doctor Shrewsberry," Reginald said.

Reginald felt relief mixed with depression after they walked out of the asylum.

"I don't know how they expect anyone could ever improve in a place like that," Alexis said.

"I do not think healing was the top priority when this hospital was built Alexis, but I suppose it was all Claire could afford," Reginald said gloomily.

"But I thought she was a movie star?"

"Yes, but Claire spent money much faster than she ever earned it," he said.

Murder By Plane 101.

"You know what they always say. Like father, like daughter," Alexis laughed mirthlessly.

"Do you think we will be able to find Claire or her father, Reggie?" She asked.

"We have these addresses to go on and all we can do is try them," he said.

"We can always find Joe's drinking establishment. Gladys said he was homeless and she called him a bum. He may spend most of his time there," she said.

"Okay, then it's another gin mill," Reginald puffed. "I hope we have better luck than we did at the last joint. My ribs are still sore."

"I'm not thrilled about going to that part of town either," she said as they seated themselves in the Duesenberg.

"Well, at least I have my trusty pistol with me this time," he said.

"I hope you don't have to use that thing," she said.

They found the ugly, turn of the century, brick building where Bernie's bar and grill had been located since before prohibition. The place was literally a hole in the wall, partially hidden in the back of the building's cellar and below street level. This had been useful during the years when alcoholic beverages were illegal. A narrow alleyway was the only ingress to the rat infested gin mill.

"This just keeps getting more and more fun Reggie," Alexis said sarcastically. "I'm glad you decided to have Dominic drive the car this time."

"I do not think it a good idea for you to accompany me into a place like this Alexis. If you will wait in the car, Dominic and I will proceed on this foray," Reginald said.

"If you insist, but I don't feel much safer in the car," Alexis said.

"If some suspicious character bothers you just lay on the horn and Dominic and I will come running. We will not be far away, my girl," he assured her.

"All right, that does sound logical and besides; I drew too much attention at the last bar," she said.

"Yes, this is definitely considered to be a man's bar and they don't get many pretty faces in there I'm sure," Reginald said.

"Why, thank you Reggie," she smiled.

"You know what I mean, Kansas." He poked her cheek with his index finger.

"Yeah, I know what you mean Mr. St. John." She batted her long lashes teasingly.

"Right then. Here we go. Are you ready Dominic?"

"I ready boss." Dominic cracked his oversized knuckles.

Alexis felt a strange since of dread as she watched the unevenly matched pair disappear around the corner of the building.

Chapter 10.

Reginald and Dominic rounded the corner of the decrepit building and found a small sign with a single name, 'Bernie's', hand painted on it. An arrow pointed to a stairway leading down to a grimy well. Broken bottles and other rubbish covered the filthy cement floor. To the left was a boarded up door with an unreadable sign.

The men stood, hesitantly, looking down the narrow stairway. Reginald looked over at the big Italian and arched his eyebrows in a mental shrug. "This is the address given to me by Mrs. Fisk. Perhaps we should inquire around the neighborhood, providing we are able to find anyone to talk to us."

"Yeah boss, we ask around. We find somebody. They gonna talk."

"Well, I suppose we should begin with the area closest to this dive and work our way out," Reginald said.

They walked further back between the old structures looking for any sign of life. Rats scurried into the dark spaces behind garbage cans and boxes.

"Remind me to take two showers when I finally get back home Dominic. I haven't been in this sort of place since the war, nor had I planned on ever going into this type of situation ever again."

"Okay boss."

They found a small ragtag cluster of men standing together near an alley entrance with their smokes. They were obviously out of work, mostly older fellows, who had nothing better to do with their time. The two were closely eyed as they approached, but not with hostility. The look in those sad faces was more defeat than aggression and Reginald felt sympathy for them. He had seen that look before in the eyes of defeated soldiers from both sides.

"Hello men," he saluted with a wave as they walked up.

The group stared back with a few mumbled greetings and half-hearted waves.

"We were looking for a bar called Bernie's. Does anyone here know of such a place?"

"It's closed Mister. Been closed fer two weeks now," one of the men said.

"Oh, so the boarded up door, around the building, was Bernie's?"

"Yeah, that's the place, "the man stepped away from the others. "Could you spare some change for a veteran Mister?"

Reginald ignored the question for now. "Perhaps you could help us find someone."

"Who?" He looked at Reginald's fine apparel and glanced over at Dominic.

"Joe Fisk," the actor replied.

Reginald was watching the man's face closely and could see the recognition.

"I might know him. What's it about? You the cops or something?"

"No, we are not with the police. Do you know where Mr.Fisk can be found?"

"Well." The man scratched his rough chin and looked at his shoes.

Reginald reached in his wallet, took out a dollar and handed it over. This caused the others to move closer, but Dominic stepped forward and they stopped short.

"Joe Fisk?" the man asked.

"Yes, Joe Fisk," Reginald replied.

"I remember him from Bernie's place. He was a regular. I tended bar there, sometimes, on busy nights."

"Do you know where we might find him?"

The man turned to the group behind him. "Any of you guys seen Joe Fisk lately?"

"I saw him a couple a weeks ago. He was hard up. Beggin for grub money," another one of the group said.

"Did you speak to him?" Reginald asked.

"We talked some. Not much. Nothin much goin on to talk about."

"Did Joe ever tell you where he resided?"
"Huh?"
"Did he say where he might be staying?"
"Nope," the man said with a small shrug.
The ex-bartender turned back to Reginald. "I just remembered something about Joe, Mister. "He was always talkin about how he was goin to the desert."
"The desert?" Reginald asked in surprise.
"Yes sir. That's what he said. He wanted to go to the Mojave desert ta find gold."
"You mean like a prospector?" Reginald asked.
"That's it," he pointed. "Prospector. Old Joe used to talk my ear off about that stuff. He said he was a prospector back in the nineties and knew all about it. He said he was sick of this city life. He was tired of not havin no money. I guess we all are, at that."
Reginald looked over at Dominic. "A prospector." Reginald stood silent for several minutes, deep in thought, then he continued.
"Do you think he has gone to the desert?"
"Well sir, he ain't around here," the man stated.
"Yes, this is true. I wonder how he can be reached now." Reginald asked.
"I guess you got to go look in the desert," the scruffy man laughed nervously.
"I suppose you are correct. Have you any idea where he might be in the desert?"
"Barstow. Yeah, I remember him talkin about it."
"You have been a great help to us. Thank you," Reginald said.
Reginald removed a handful of cash from his wallet and gave each man in the group five dollars. Dominic followed closely to make sure no one became too eager. Reginald warned them of the possibility a dangerous man might be looking for information about Joe Fisk. The men all assured Reginald that the whereabouts of Joe was safe within their ranks.

106. T.E.Avery

"It is sad to see good men in such a state," Reginald replied, after he and Dominic had walked away.

"Yeah boss. That true. Sad," Dominic nodded his large head.

Alexis had been sitting alone in the car for over twenty minutes. Her blouse was beginning to stick to her back and the hot breeze didn't help. She quickly became hot, bored, and unnerved by the occasional onlookers who stopped and stared at the car and her. The thought occurred to her these folks were not used to seeing such an expensive automobile parked in their neighborhood. She sat in the backseat fanning herself with an old studio bulletin. "I wish they would hurry up," she muttered.

She tried not to notice the passersby and as she turned her head to find something to look at, she happened to see a black car parked down the street. It was too far away, but the car seemed strangely familiar to her. Someone was sitting in the driver's seat watching her. She couldn't tell if it was a man or a woman from this distance, but the car resembled the one that almost ran into them at the studio the other night and didn't Dominic say the car that came for Greta was black? She had nothing else to do and it wouldn't hurt to check it out. She got out of the car and climbed into the driver's seat.

As the duo rounded the side of the building they were stunned to find the car and Alexis were gone. Both men stood at the curb looking up and down the street. Reginald felt momentarily confused and a strange feeling of loss, followed by fear, swept over him.

"Where the car boss?"

"That's a good question Dominic. I wonder what has happened?"

"Miss Moxley take the car for a drive, I guess. I leave the keys with her just like you told me boss."

"That was supposed to be in case of an emergency only. I have never actually seen her drive an automobile

Murder By Plane 107.

Dominic and I'm not sure she even has her license."

"I never seen her drive before too. What we gonna do now?" Dominic said, scratching his head in perplexity.

"I don't know Dominic. I suppose we will have to stand here for a while and see if she turns up." Reginald was mentally fighting a growing sense of anxiety. He looked around and saw that there were several men and women nearby.

"Perhaps one of those people will be able to tell us something." He walked over to a man of undeterminable age, sitting on a bench.

"Hello my good man, perhaps you can provide some assistance to us," Reginald said cheerfully. The fellow looked startled as he had not noticed their approach. "We seem to have mislaid an automobile that was parked here," Reginald continued.

The man stared at Reginald for several seconds. "You mean that high falootin jalopy with the knockout dame in it?" The man asked.

Reginald turned to Dominic and shrugged.

"He say he seen the car boss," Dominic translated.

"Did you happen to notice in which direction the lady drove the automobile sir?"

The fellow, again, stared at Reginald as if he didn't understand.

"Which way she go?" Dominic asked.

"Oh, that broad got the hot foot fer sure. Took off lickety split after another heap."

"I do not understand you, sir." Reginald's entire face was a question mark.

"Ain't ma fault you're a long haired stuffed shirt," the man replied rudely.

"You watch your mouth boy." Dominic started to close in with fists bunched. The smaller man stood to run away.

It was at this time they heard a familiar horn honking and turned to see Alexis pull up in the Duesenberg.

"Hi boys." She had a smile on her face and an ice cream cone melting in her hand. "It's not easy to drive this machine with one hand."

"Where have you been?" Reginald tried to control his emotions. He felt angry and relieved at the same time. Part of him wanted to scold her and the other part wanted to rush over and put his arms around her.

Alexis could sense the irritation in his voice, but she attempted to change the subject as she got out of the car licking the cone. "Who is that man you were talking to?"
Reginald and Dominic both turned to the bench, but the man was long gone.

"It doesn't matter now. Let's be off before a crowd gathers round," Reginald said.

"I got so warm sitting here in the car. I hope you don't mind me borrowing it for a little while. Do you want a lick?" she smiled and held up what was left of the cone.

Reginald looked at the melting vanilla ice cream and the small amount on her top lip.

"No thanks," he replied dryly, but minus the irritation.

"Where we go now boss?"
Reginald's attention strayed from the girl sitting next to him.

"Well, now that Mr. Fisk is out of our reach at present, I suppose we should follow up on those addresses we were given earlier today."

"What do you mean out of reach?" Her pink tongue removed the remaining ice cream from her mouth.

Reginald tried not to show his fascination with her moist lips. "Apparently, he has left the city."

"Do you know where he has gone?"

"According to a fellow who knew him from the bar he frequented, Joe Fisk has become a gold prospector in the Mojave desert."

"A what?"

"A gold prospector."

Murder By Plane 109.

She could tell by his clipped sentences that he was still somewhat irritated. She didn't understand if it was fear for her safety or something else.

"I didn't know people still did that sort of thing. Are you sure the information you received is reliable?"

"I'm not sure of anything at this moment, but all we can do is proceed with what we have to go on, unless you can think of something better to do. Maybe we should go find some cotton candy to go with the ice cream," he said sarcastically.

"Look. I got too hot and I was bored. If you're mad at me then just say so." Her eyes glistened with the beginnings of tears. "And besides, I saw a car parked down the street that looked like the one we saw coming out of the backlot the night we found Brogan dead. Someone was sitting there watching us and when I drove down the street they turned around and sped off lickety-split."

"Oh. Sorry, my girl. I suppose I was just a little worried about you. Did you get a look at the person in the car?"

"No," she pouted.

He had trouble taking his eyes off her incredible mouth. He inwardly chastised himself for having these lustful feelings for someone so much younger than himself. She had almost been his sister-in-law too.

Several hours later they had exhausted themselves and their list of addresses. They had gone over to Claire Cauldwell's last known place of residence and then her father's place.

They had also checked the apartment that Greta had given as her home address, but the woman who answered the door had never heard of a Greta Muiller. After they checked out the last lead they decided it was time to take a break and have something to eat at Reginald's favorite diner. Alexis and Reginald were seated at his favorite semi-private booth, but Dominic insisted on taking his sandwich back to the car.

"I don't understand it Reggie. All of these fake addresses. She took the last bite of her roast beef sandwich. What's going on here anyway?"

"I don't know either. I am beginning to see we have found pieces to a puzzle, but we just cannot fit them together yet. Why, for instance, would Greta give a false address unless she was hiding something?"

"Yeah. And why would she run away unless she was guilty of something?"

"I wonder what she has done that would make her run away from us? As a matter of fact, she started in my employment at the time of Claire's release from the mental hospital."

"So?. What are you trying to say Reggie? That Claire Cauldwell and Greta Muiller are the same person?"

"They were approximately the same height and Claire is an actress. She may not have been that great in the talkies, but she knew about costumes."

"Oh wow. I think you may have solved a piece of the puzzle. I wonder where she went? Could she have gone to the Mojave desert with her old man?"

"Not Claire. She would never leave until she got what she wanted from me. I can only guess what she was up to by disguising herself like that. Also, did she plot and carry out the hit and run accident that injured poor Grace so she could come along as the Austrian cook at the opportune time? I am of the mind it is time to visit the Los Angeles Police Department and find someone who will believe our tale of intrigue and assassinations."

"Yeah, what you said." She drank the last of her iced tea as the radio played a familiar song by Hoagy Carmichael.

It was several hours later and the sun was beginning to go down when they finished talking to the police at the main precinct. Reginald's status in the community had gotten them in where most citizens would have been turned away.

Murder By Plane 111.

They had found a busy detective Sergeant Atkins, who told them he was looking into Frank Brogan's death as foul play, but he was reluctant to discuss any details about the case. He listened to their side of the story, minus the fact that they had been at the studio that night, but said he could see no link between Frank Brogan's death, the studio fire, the airplane crash and the break-in at Mrs. Fisk's place.

He told them the fire investigators had found out the blaze was caused by a faulty electrical cord on an old desk lamp. It had been ruled an accident by the Fire Marshal. They left the police station feeling like two kids with over- zealous imaginations.

"I was only in the file room for a few minutes, but I don't remember seeing any desks or desk lamps in there," Alexis said. They were in the backseat as Dominick drove them toward the studio airfield in the hopes of finding the aircraft mechanic Don Denison.

"Perhaps it was on the floor and you did not have the time to notice it."

"Maybe. But why would they have an old desk lamp in there when there was plenty of modern overhead lighting?" Alexis asked.

"That is a good question, my girl, and one that we may never find out."

"I hate it when people treat me like I'm just a dumb blonde. That detective should have believed our story Reggie."

"Yes, I agree with you, but unfortunately, the police deal in facts only. They are not likely to reopen the sabotage case until we find more facts ourselves."

"But the detective you hired got murdered and someone burned the storeroom the same night. That should have gotten someone's attention," she said.

"Yes, you would think so, but we still need more pieces to the puzzle in order to convince the police. They have too much to do and not enough men to waste in fruitless searching."

"Hey, whose side are you on anyway?" She sounded irritated and he knew she probably felt tired and frustrated. Her hair and makeup looked slightly wilted, but she was still very beautiful to gaze upon, he thought to himself. He gently patted her hand.

"We will go over to the hanger and have a talk with Don Denison about the aircraft. The police report made mention of some missing tools taken from Don's tool chest the night before my crash. He told the police that these were the tools needed to remove a wheel from the aircraft."

"And the report also said the tools were never recovered. That was why the Department of Transportation and the police had investigated it as a possible sabotage. I wonder why they gave up on it?"

"I believe it was lack of further evidence to prove otherwise."

"You mean it was easier to prove an accident than to prove sabotage."

Again he could detect the anger in her tone. She was so different than Lillian. So much resemblance on the outside, yet so dissimilar on the inside. Lillian had been almost delicate in her constitution and could never have kept up a grueling pace in the heat this way, but Alexis seemed to be coping with it as best she could. He tried to cheer her as they approached the airfield.

"Perhaps you would enjoy a nice swim in the ocean later?"

"At night?"

"Yes, we could take a stroll down the beach and a moonlight dip."

"That sounds grand." She smiled and continued to fan herself with the battered bulletin as Dominic parked the car in the same place he had several nights ago. Reginald thought he could hear the roaring of an aircraft engine coming from inside the hanger.

Chapter 11.

Dominic remained with the automobile as Reginald and Alexis walked toward the back of the large hanger. Reginald listened to the familiar sound of the Nieuport's 240.C engine, droning steadily inside the cavity of the building.

"Don must be tuning up the engine. It seems strange he would be doing it so late in the day."

"Why is it strange?" Alexis asked.

"They do not usually run the motors for so long inside the hanger because of the fumes. It is mostly done earlier in the day outside the front doors. Those exhaust fumes can really be murder." As soon as the words came out of his mouth they looked at each other.

"Reggie, you don't think…?" She left the question hanging as the aircraft engine sputtered and gasped as it finally gave up and died. The eerie silence was unnerving as they approached the outer door.

"You better let me check inside first," he whispered as he took out the pistol.

"What if I go in behind you with the flashlight ready?" He could see her hand trembling as she held the light.

"All right, but the fumes could be overpowering. Leave this door wide open while I take a quick look inside."

As Reginald stepped into the opening he could smell the engine exhaust and unburned gasoline in the air. The overhead lights were on and he could see that the big front doors were closed. He knew there had to be something wrong if Don was running the aircraft engine with the building closed up. The fumes were not as bad as expected and he motioned for the girl to come inside.

"Hello. Don? Are you here Don?" Reginald called out from the rear entrance.

The overhead lights caused the hanger to become a surreal place of light and dark. Shadowy nooks and crannies were everywhere, while bright beams burned through the darkness elsewhere. As before, the Nieuport stood in its usual spot facing the front doors. The ribs could be seen through the cloth of the beautiful upper wing, but the smaller lower wing remained hidden in darkness, as was the undercarriage.

They followed the same path as before and went around the plane from behind. Reginald intended to get over to the double doors and open them in order to further clear the air. He slowly stepped around the left wing of the aircraft and saw that something was terribly wrong. An unmistakably large amount of blood covered the floor. Reginald had not seen that much blood since the war. He began to experience the feeling of stalling in an airplane. The fumes had dissipated considerably and the coppery smell of blood could be detected in the air. He stopped moving and Alexis stood close to him with her hand on his back.

"Reggie? What's wrong? Are you okay?"

Her voice brought him out of his mental fog and he quickly turned around to face her. She could see Reginald's ashen face and his hand felt clammy as he took hold of hers.

"Stay here," he said quietly.

"What's happened?" The wing and the deep shadow it cast under the plane kept her from viewing the sight he had just experienced.

"Alexis, you must not move from this spot. I will go around to the front of the airplane and take a look, but we cannot touch anything or move around in this hanger." She could see the color had returned to his face and he had a look of grim determination.

Reginald carefully avoided the gore as he slowly inched forward, his eyes scanning the smooth cement floor.

Don's body lay against the far wall of the hanger with a trail of blood leading back to the nose of the Nieuport. Reginald could see that Don's left arm had been severed, partially hidden under the plane. He walked to the front of the hanger and closely inspected the area. Finding nothing there, he walked back around the wing section to find Alexis standing where he had instructed. She had intuited that something horrible had occurred and took his orders seriously this time.

"What did you see Reggie?"

"You don't want to know the details, my girl. It looks as if the Nieuport has killed again. We need to vacate this charnel house and call the police."

"Is it Don? Did the exhaust fumes kill him?"

"No, not the exhaust fumes. The propeller."

"Oh God," Alexis exclaimed.

As they made their way back to the rear of the hanger and into the fresh air, Reginald noticed something on the doorstep. Alexis turned back to see what he was inspecting.

"What did you find?"

"It looks like a scrap of office notepaper someone could have dropped as they left. Perhaps when they were reaching into a pocket for keys," Reginald said.

"How could you conclude all that from one tiny scrap of paper?" she asked.

"Because it has a smudge of blood on it and some numbers."

"Are you going to pick it up?"

"No. We need to call the police and tell them everything we have seen tonight. After this they just may believe our story and reopen the case."

They had found their way to a security shack where they convinced the guard to let them use the phone to call the police. First, Reginald had to explain what they had been doing on the studio property and what they had found.

Reginald and Alexis stood near the back door of the hanger explaining their story to detective Sergeant Atkins again. Atkins and several uniformed officers made it to the backlot in less than an hour after the call was made. One officer had even asked Reginald for his autograph, only to be chastised by the Sergeant.

Sergeant Atkins and the officer then went into the building to inspect the scene. Reginald pointed out the notepaper evidence on the floor. Ten minutes later, they exited the building. The younger cop looked shaky and pale in the dim light outside the hanger. It wasn't long before he lost his dinner at the side of the building. Sergeant Atkins shook his head and chuckled to himself.

"If he had been in the war, stuff like that wouldn't shock him so," Atkins said.

"It is a bloody way to die you must admit Sergeant."

"Yeah, I guess so, Mr. St. John. I suppose the poor fellow accidentally walked into the prop and bled to death, right on the floor, after it took his arm off."

"Yes, or perhaps he was pushed into the propeller by someone," Reginald said.

"Oh, not likely Mr. St. John. I'm thinking it must have been accidental."

"Why would he have the plane running in a closed hanger detective?"

"I don't know. Maybe you better tell me," The sergeant said irritably.

"What about the scrap of paper I showed you?" Reginald asked.

"Look Mr. St. John. I know it was kind of tough for you to see the guy messed up and all, but please don't start telling the police how to run an investigation. Why don't you two go on home now and get some rest. I'll get in touch if I need anything further from you and please call me if you remember anything else."

Reginald stared into the Sergeant's eyes and tried to remain as calm as possible; given the circumstances and the long day he and Alexis had been through. He tried not to think about all the leg work they had done for the cops. Now this wind bag was telling him to go home to bed like a kid being patted on the head.

He began to talk in a low steady monotone voice that soon had the detective yawning and rubbing his eyes. Alexis, standing beside him, began to feel the effects of

Murder By Plane 117.
his calming speech too. She fought the urge to find a place to sit down, her legs began feeling heavy. She could hardly make out what Reginald was telling the sergeant, but she thought it had something to do with making sure a thorough search had been performed and the scene had not been contaminated. He also reminded the sergeant to dust for fingerprints. Strangely, the normally brash policeman stood patiently until the actor finished, and then he turned to his men, repeating everything Reginald had just told him, word for word. Reginald grabbed Alexis by the wrist and led her to the Duesenberg.

"That will teach him to talk down to us, my girl," he said as they slid into the backseat. Dominic slammed the door.

"What did you just do Reggie?"

"Nothing much. I was only reminding the good Sergeant of his duties."

Her eyes opened wide now and she was pointing her finger at him. "You did that voice trick-thing again, didn't you? And on a policeman too."

By the time they reached Reginald's home Alexis was slumped against his shoulder fast asleep. Reginald looked down at the top of her blonde head and her small hands as she slept. How childlike she seemed to him now. Dominic insisted on carrying the sleeping girl into the house and making her comfortable on a leather sofa in the living room. She could easily spend the entire night there without a sore neck or back in the morning. After the burly Italian had gone, Reginald slipped her shoes from her feet and loosened her top buttons. He went into the study to unwind with a shot of scotch, thinking about all that had occurred today.

The killer was hiding his tracks so well even the police were convinced everything that had happened, from the plane crash a year ago, to Don Denison's grisly death today, was accidental. What about Claire or Greta, if that was who she was pretending to be? What role was she playing in all of this? Surely Claire could not have been the one who has carried out this string of murders which were so cleverly planned and completed. Possibly her mind had snapped so completely that Claire really believed she was someone else, or maybe she is an accomplice spying for the mastermind who was behind it all. He knew the puzzle would never come together until they found Joe Fisk.

Fisk was the only one who could identify the murderer and free Reginald from the guilt and self loathing that tormented his soul. He poured another shot of the scotch and sat down at his desk, forcing himself to write, before retiring for the night.

Later that night, Alexis was awakened from a deep sleep by the sound of a man's shout. At first she was confused about the time and place before realizing she had been sleeping on a leather sofa fully clothed. She lay as still as possible and tried to listen for the noise again, but no other sounds could be heard. After several minutes, which seemed like hours, she decided to investigate rather than go back to sleep. Sitting up on the edge of the sofa, she put her bare feet on the floor. Reginald or Dominic must have carried her into the house and put her on the soft leather sofa. She didn't remember falling asleep, but knew she must have, especially after Reginald's display of hypnosis on the police sergeant. Suddenly, another sharp scream cut through the darkness and Alexis realized it was coming from Reginald's quarters, upstairs.

"What time is it?" She murmured to herself as she tried to keep from breaking her knee on a nearby table. The moonlight shone across the room through the blinds and she knew it was either very late at night or very early in the morning. Alexis carefully navigated her way over to the stairs and began to ascend into the spooky darkness. All sorts of frightening thoughts occurred to her as she ascended the stairs. What if the killer had broke into the house and was going from room to room with a large knife? Maybe he had not noticed her sleeping on the dark sofa, and after looking in her empty bedroom, had gone after Reginald upstairs. Her hand was involuntarily shaking on the banister and her legs felt like jelly. I've got to pull myself together. If that was Reginald's scream, then surely he was in trouble and needed her assistance. She wished she had looked around for something to use for a weapon. She came to the top of the stairs. Alexis noticed Reginald's door was open.

A few minutes later Reginald felt a hand press against his chest in the dark. He had been awake for several minutes after having the familiar nightmare and could see the figure in the moonlight moving noiselessly across the room. At first, still confused by the dream and groggy from sleep, he was sure it must be Lillian's ghost.

"Alexis."

"Reggie?" she whispered.

"I'm awake. What are you doing up here?"

"Thank God you're okay. I heard you scream and thought something happened to you or the killer broke in." Her hand was now on his arm as she knelt on the floor.

"No. It's just a recurring nightmare I have had for the last few months. I am sorry it woke you." He was now sitting up in bed rubbing his eyes.

"No, its okay. I was just a little frightened," she lied.

"Do you know what time it is?" He held his bedside clock up to the moonlight shining through the window.

"It's late, but I feel too wound up to go back to bed now." She walked over to the open French doors that led to his balcony. The surf gently hissed below.

"Me too. And I have a headache to boot."

"Why don't we sit out on the balcony and enjoy the cool air. I could massage your shoulders for you. I'm good at it."

"Do you have a lot of experience rubbing men's

shoulders in their bedrooms?" He joined her outside and they sat on the comfortable wicker chairs.

"No silly." She tried not to take offence. "I took care of my father when he was sick. Didn't Lillian ever tell you about it?"

"She never talked about her past very much; now that you mention it," he replied.

The balcony overlooked the Pacific Ocean and the view, with the moonlight shining across the ever moving waves, was incredible. Reginald felt himself relax as Alexis's fingers rubbed his neck muscles. She began to tell him her story in a quiet soothing voice.

"Mother died when we were young and Dad got sick about a year after Lillian moved away. It was all up to me to take care of him and manage the house too. Lillian came home from time to time, but only to visit, and it usually made more work for me. I had to take care of everything."

"I am sorry Alexis." He lightly stroked the back of her hand.

"No. It's okay really." Her voice broke and a small sob escaped.

"Your father was a very lucky man to have a daughter like you to take care of him."

"Thanks Reggie. I just did what any girl would do in the same situation." She continued her ministrations, having recovered emotionally.

"How did you manage it all?" He shook his head. "Weren't there any other relations that could provide assistance?"

"No. Just me. I suppose that's why I seem so bold and brassy at times. I had to learn to take charge of everything and to be a fighter. I was always the Tomboy anyway. Lillian was the girly girl.
If there was a fight with the neighbor kids I was always in the middle of it, even though I was six years younger." She laughed quietly, but her seriousness

Murder By Plane 121.

returned quickly. "After Dad was gone, Lillian and I agreed the house should be sold and I would go to college. I went into drama, of course."

She looked out at the beautiful scene before them as the bright moon began to set and night birds circled over the beach with piercing cries. She had never been in a more romantic setting.

"Now I am the one who has been mesmerized," he said with a laugh.

Reginald rose slowly from his chair. Turning to Alexis, he took her hand and stared into her eyes. They appeared gray in the moonlight, just as her sister's had looked. She gazed back at him expectantly. She wanted to be held in his arms, but the spell was broken and the moment lost by her resemblance to Lillian in the moonlight.

"It is getting late. I suppose we better get some sleep, my girl." He dropped his eyes and patted her hand. "Thank you. You really are an amazing woman Alexis." Down on the beach, Claire Cauldwell stood quietly in the shadows with clenched fists. She watched as the two went back into the house.

Chapter 12.

The next day, after lunch, Reginald and Alexis were sitting in Max Carver's cramped office listening to the lawyer explain his findings concerning Greta Muiller. Reginald called his lawyer that morning to ask him about his inquiries regarding the former cook.

"I made every effort to find information about Greta Muiller, but I'm afraid I've hit a dead end."

"You mean she was never listed with emigration?" Reginald asked.

"No. She wasn't listed anywhere. It's like she never existed at all. Very unusual."

"Do you think she could have been someone else posing as Greta?"

"You mean like a fake identity?"

"Well yes, and no, Max. We think Greta Muiller was really Claire Cauldwell. She was disguising herself as Greta."

"Say again?"

"Do you remember Claire Cauldwell? The actress?"

"Claire Cauldwell? Hmmm. Let me think. Oh. Okay. The young actress that vanished a few years ago."

"That's the one. We believe she was acting as Greta."

"That sounds rather absurd Reg. Why would she pose as your cook?"

"We discovered, from a reliable source, Claire was psychologically unbalanced and had been in and out of the State Mental Hospital. She released herself on the same date Greta inquired about the job as my cook."

"Coincidence. It just doesn't make sense to me. What would she want from you?"

"Perhaps she was planted in my house as a spy. We also think the automobile accident that Grace Robinson, my original cook, was involved in, wasn't an accident at all. We think someone set Grace up for that wreck to get her out of my house and Greta, or Claire, if you will, was sent as a replacement," Reginald said.

Murder By Plane 123.

The lawyer leaned back in his chair and mopped his brow with the back of his hand.

"This is like a movie plot. Are you sure of any of this Reg? Have you been to the police?"

"We went to the police and they didn't believe it either," Alexis added.

"Have you made any other inquiries that could be of help to us in any way Max?" Reginald asked.

"I did find out something interesting about Bruno Von Heller that you may think fascinating," the lawyer said.

"I doubt anything about Von Heller would fascinate us," Reginald stated.

"This will, I'm sure Reg." Max was rubbing his hands together.

"Tell us your great revelation." Reginald spread his arms dramatically.

"Were you aware that Bruno Von Heller had a younger brother who remained in Germany when Bruno came to this country?"

"No. But what has this to do with us?" Reginald was getting impatient and wanted out of the hot office.

"His brother fought for Germany in the war, Reg."

"So what, Max? Millions fought in the war," Reginald said.

"He was a fighter pilot killed in a dogfight," the lawyer said.

"Oh, well that is sad, but I still do not see what it has to do with me."

"It happened over the French countryside, near the city of Reims, on March, 15 1918. Now are we getting closer Reg?" Max was smiling.

"What is he trying to say Reggie?" Alexis noticed Reginald's complexion had paled. He had a vacant look on his face. "Reggie, what does it mean? Tell me." She placed her hand on his arm. He looked down at her hand when she increased her grip. Now he was looking into her eyes.

"I killed his brother," Reginald said.

"But how could you know that? She looked over at Carver, who was now leaning forward. How could anyone know that?" she asked.

"I was in that dogfight Alexis. I remember it as if it were just yesterday. I shot down a single German plane on that day," Reginald said.

"But how do you know it was you who killed his brother? Are you sure it wasn't someone else?" she asked.

Reginald looked from Alexis to his former squadron comrade and back again.

"Because there were no others, my girl," he stated flatly.

"You mean you were flying alone?" she asked.

"Yes. I was on dawn patrol. It could only have been me," Reginald replied.

"That would give Von Heller a motive for …." She began.

"Revenge," Carver finished.

"Revenge and murder," Alexis said. "Von Heller had the motive and the opportunity to cause your plane to crash Reggie."

"He also had the method. The plane was so near the studio it would have been easy for him to get his hands on it," Reginald said.

"Maybe he hired someone to do it and then he eliminated that person," Alexis stated.

"Don Denison," Reginald added.

Carver interrupted their excited comments.

"Did you ever locate the witness you were talking about the last time you were here?"

"We found out where he may have gone Max. All we need to do is go and speak to him in person, but we have not had time."

"So you know where he is hiding?" Carver asked.

"Yes, we found out he has become a gold prospector in the Mojave desert of all places," Reginald said.

"A gold prospector? You mean the fellows who walk around with a mule?" Carver chuckled and took a pipe and tobacco out of a desk drawer. "Do you mind?"

Alexis thought there was something different about the desk.

"Not at all." Alexis hated tobacco smoke, but knew they would be leaving soon.

"So you haven't talked to the one witness and the police won't listen to you? Maybe its time to throw in the towel and get on with your lives now," Carver stated.

"That's why we are caught up in this case Mr. Carver. We must find out who killed my sister before we can rest."

Carver looked from Alexis to Reginald.

"I'm with her in this until the bitter end Max," Reginald said.

"Well I hope it's not a bitter end Reg. Especially if Bruno Von Heller is involved. What are you going to do now that you have this new information about Bruno?"

"I don't really know Max. Perhaps we should go to Bruno and confront him with it in order to rattle his chain and see what happens," Reginald said.

"You both better be very careful, and keep me posted," the lawyer said.

Reginald decided he needed a drink after hearing this latest revelation about Bruno Von Heller's brother, so they headed for home after leaving Max Carver's office.

"Reggie, how could Max Carver have found out about Von Heller's brother?"

"Clyde knows a lot of people Alexis. I'm sure it was reliable information, but he would never reveal his sources to anyone," Reginald said.

"Clyde?"

"Yes, remember I told you Max is just his nickname," Reginald said.

"What sort of man is he Reggie?"

"You mean on a personal level?"

"Yeah. What was he like during the war?"

"He was more serious than the rest of us, but he was always a good friend. Sometimes he seemed to be competing with me over how many Germans we could kill."

"That sounds brutal."

"It was brutal, my girl. It was war."

"But how do you know for sure that you killed Von Heller's brother? What if he parachuted out at the last moment?" she asked.

"Because there were no parachutes," Reginald stated.

"You mean they hadn't been invented yet?" she asked.

"Oh yes, parachutes have been around for a long time, but the war offices on either side would not issue them to flyers," he said.

"What? why not?"

"They said it was bad for morale. It might imply something could go wrong. The only problem was something always did go wrong," he laughed without humor.

Back at the beach villa they were enjoying a cool glass of wine on the veranda, overlooking the Ocean. Reginald's drinking had slowed since he and Alexis started working on the investigation. He felt, however, a small amount of alcohol was needed after hearing the revelation concerning Von Heller's brother and all the talk about the war.

"Now we just need to find a way to get close to Von Heller and get him talking," Alexis said.

"Yes, that should be a simple task I'm sure," Reginald stated sarcastically.

"I know what you mean, but there has to be a way to get close to that creep or to find someone who is already close to him. I thought you still had contacts at the studio?"

"Oh I do, but none of whom have been involved with someone like Bruno."

Murder By Plane 127.

"Did my sister have any friends who were closely associated with Von Heller?"

"There may have been one or two, but no one I would place any trust in. There were many actresses who would have been glad to see Lillian fail. It seems as though the more a person gains success in life, the more people try to bring him or her down."

"Or eliminate them?" she said.

"Perhaps," he took a long drink. "But this still doesn't solve our problem of finding out Von Heller's role in the crimes."

"What do you really know about him Reggie?" Alexis asked.

"Not very much. I mostly know about him from the way he behaved on the set. I have been to one or two parties he also attended. There is something about the way you feel when you walk away from the man. I can't quite put my finger on it."

"I know exactly what you mean. He makes you feel like you need to wash the evil off." She cringed.

"Yes, that is an excellent way to describe it, my girl," he said.

"Hey Reggie, I just had an idea that could work," Alexis said excitedly.

"Do you mean a better idea for describing the evil nature of Bruno Von Heller?" he said jokingly.

"No. To get closer to him so we can somehow get him to admit his involvement in Lillian's death," she said.

His face became more serious now. "What are you thinking Alexis?"

"I could audition for a part, however small, in one of his movies and once in the Studio, I turn on the charm and try to get close to him." She finished with a smile and a flourish of her hand.

"Oh, just like that. Do you honestly think a man like Von Heller would not see through your scheme? Do you know how dangerous that man could be Alexis? Do you

128. *T.E.Avery*
want your life in peril and no one around to help you. I cannot allow it."

"Have you got any other ideas Reggie?" She took his hand in both of hers and looked deeply into his eyes. "I am willing to do whatever it takes to find the person who killed my sister and if it means placing myself in danger, then so be it. You have been so good to me and you have protected me during all of this, but now I have to go onto the stage alone."

"This could be your last act Alexis," he said mirthlessly.

"Or maybe my grand finale." She tried to smile, but felt a hard knot in her stomach and light-headedness at the thought of confronting the man who was probably responsible for her sister's death.

Bruno Von Heller saw himself as the center of the universe. The flabby bald man sat behind an immense and incredibly elaborate, mahogany desk reading a script for his latest production. His personal retainers stood at various, appointed, spots around the room. Their order determined by rank in the bizarre little world of Von Heller. At Bruno's right elbow sat his personal secretary, Sidney.

Sidney was a man so small and effeminate most people had to guess if he were male or female. He clutched a pen and pad, at the ready for Von Heller's instructions. Another minion knelt at his side holding the script, while a manicurist put the finishing touches on Von Heller's nails.

The script writer stood in front of the desk waiting as his boss approved, or in this case, mostly disapproved his latest efforts. He had been standing for over an hour, although a comfortable chair stood nearby. The writer had not been asked to sit and everyone knew, in Bruno's universe, Bruno decided who sat and who didn't. "Did you get all of those changes, Sidney?" Bruno examined his fingers and signaled for the manicurist to leave.

Murder By Plane

"Yes, Mr. Von Heller. Just as you want them sir."

"I was able to salvage that trash, this time, at least. I surprise myself with my own brilliance at times." He snickered in an ugly way and the others, except the writer, joined him.

"Now get back to work. We have a deadline to make and time is money," Bruno was now satisfied he had successfully humiliated the man in front of everyone. He knew the writer, or any of his other employees, would never find another job in Hollywood if he quit. Bruno would make sure of that. He watched with pleasure as the man left the room with his shoulders drooping.

The morning after her decision to audition for a part in Bruno Von Heller's production, Alexis was in her room adding the finishing touches to her makeup and hair. She decided to wear her silk oriental patterned dress and matching accessories. It was all the rage. Would sandals or heels be best to show off her delicate ankles; heels it is.

Alexis was determined to find a way back into the studio to expose the killer of her sister. She had risen early with her plans starting to fall into shape. She knew no one at the Studio would recognize her from her previous position as secretary. She had changed her looks enough to solve that problem and this time she would be using her real name.

The house had been unusually quiet this morning. She had prepared a small breakfast and afterward, gotten herself dressed and ready for her mission. Alexis began to experience a tug of anxiety at the thought of going back to that place. She wished Reginald had gotten out of bed to see her off. After she persuaded him to go along with her plan, they had agreed she would have to move into her own place. No doubt Bruno would have her watched until he was convinced she could be trusted. Reginald had secured a small apartment, for her, near the studio. He also made a call to his agent, Rance Hinds, to get the girl into Von Heller's film, making sure Rance kept everything low key and confidential. Reginald had known Rance for many years and the agent owed his own success to the movie star.

Alexis began to have second thoughts about the idea as she made her way downstairs and toward the front door. Dominic would move her into the apartment after she was sure she had gotten the role in the production. She felt very small, and afraid, as she opened the door and stepped out into the morning sun.

As soon as she exited the door and before her eyes had become accustomed to the light, a horn was honking loudly from the direction of the driveway. To her surprise, Reginald sat behind the wheel of a new Ford Roadster. He motioned her to come over for a closer look at the yellow coup. Dominic parked the larger car in the garage.

"Did you buy a new car this morning Reggie?" she asked.

"Yes. What do you think of her?
This is the automobile all the gangsters desire."

"Oh. And so now you're thinking of robbing banks?"

"No, but I thought you might need a car to get around town and besides, the   Duesenberg is too conspicuous and recognizable for our detective work."

"You mean you went out and bought this car for me?" Alexis asked.

"Yes Alexis. This is your car. You do have a driver's license don't you?"

"Yeah, but I can't accept this car Reggie. You have already done so much."

"Well, its only money, my girl. And we need it to accomplish our mission don't we?"

"Yeah, I guess so. I thought you were still in bed this morning. I was having second thoughts about our plan." She rubbed her hand along the smooth paint and chrome.

"Well I got up extra early this morning and Dominic drove me into town and we picked up this dandy little buggy." He removed his lanky form from the drivers seat. "Why don't you try it out?"

"Wow, it's beautiful. Do you mind?" she asked.

"It is your car, remember. And don't you have an audition in about twenty minutes anyway? But watch your speed, my girl. This is the fastest car on the road."

Bruno sat, surrounded by staff, as usual, in the back row of seats in the small theater. The auditions would begin soon. He brooded like a fat toad as he thought about his encounter with Reginald St.John at the premier the other night. How he hated St. John.

Now he found that the girl who had been with him was auditioning for a role in this film. The nerve of that has-been actor to interfere with one of my productions. He would humiliate the girl in front of his staff and everyone. That would teach them that no one insulted Bruno Von Heller and got away unscathed.

"I will show them," he said quietly.

"What did you say sir?" Sidney asked.

"Nothing. I was just thinking out loud."

He had found out as much as he could about Alexis Moxley after learning that she was auditioning today. He knew she had been seen around town with Reginald St. John and it was rumored they were living together. That meant Reginald probably had serious feelings for the little tramp or she would not be staying with him.

As Bruno mulled over those thoughts, a plan began to form in his mind. Why not allow the girl to get a role in the film so he could find a way to lure her away from St. John?

"Yes, that is what I will do," the fat man said.

"Excuse me sir? I didn't understand."

"Shut up, Sidney."

"Yes sir."

Chapter 13.

Reginald attempted to control his worried thoughts concerning Alexis. He was lounging on a folding chair, in the shade of a palm tree, absently watching Pedro mow the small yard. He could see Dominic washing the Duesenberg. It had been Alexis's idea after all, and Reginald knew he must wait for her return from the audition.

Dominic looked over from his chrome polishing and their eyes met for an instant. The big man shook his head slightly and resumed his duties. Dominic, with his traditional Italian values, did not approve of putting the girl in danger and he had made it known clearly to Reginald and the young actress.

This had been a bad idea from the start, Reginald thought. No one knew what a man like Von Heller could be capable of. On the other hand, with their one witness out of reach, and no other alternatives, what choice did they have? If Alexis could get the role in Von Heller's production and somehow get close enough to him to obtain a confession or secure some sort of proof from the mogul, it would be something they could bring before the police.

Reginald's mind worked in circles as he tried to justify his decision to allow Alexis to go ahead with this dangerous undertaking. He tried to think of an acquaintance that would be willing to offer help to them in some way, someone who still worked at the Studio or for Von Heller. It looked as if the girl would be flying solo on this mission and he hoped she could pull it off successfully without getting herself killed in the process. It was like flying without a parachute, since he would not be able to step in and save Alexis if something went wrong. Reginald, the realist, knew something always went wrong.

Alexis was ecstatic the audition had not only gone well, but that she actually had a major speaking role in the new film. She could hardly concentrate on her driving as she turned onto Hollywood Boulevard, barely avoiding a pedestrian. "Just wait until Reggie hears about this," she said aloud, her hands shaking and feeling clammy as she gripped the steering wheel. Alexis felt light headed as she drove the new roadster.

Now she would be able to start her own career and hopefully find out more about Von Heller's involvement in all of this. He had actually been quite nice to her as she read the part on the soundstage. She had expected him to humiliate her in front of everyone, but instead, much to her surprise, he had applauded after her small performance. Von Heller suggested she try another reading for a bigger role. Alexis nearly fainted when the producer clapped his doughy hands and complimented her.

No mention had been made of either her sister, or Reginald, and it seemed as if it could finally be her turn. She was no longer in Lillian's shadow.

Now she would get to show everyone, including Reginald, that she possessed acting abilities too. Of course, it was true she had accepted the apartment and the new car from Reginald, but she could pay him back now that her star was shining. Who knew how far she could go in the movies now that she had achieved something on her own? Alexis had a wonderful feeling of excitement she had never felt before. Then, for no apparent reason, a mental image of a young actress jumping to her death from the "HOLLYWOODLAND" sign, made her shudder involuntarily.

What made me think that?

Back in his huge office, Von Heller rubbed his small pale hands together as he contemplated the trap he had set for the gullible young actress. How easily she had fallen under the irresistible charm of Hollywood fame and fortune. All he had to do was throw out a few morsels of carefully choreographed kindness.

He snickered to himself as he pictured Reginald's reaction when he found out the girl would be under his control. The poor little creature would be an innocent pawn while she imagined her own career being launched into Hollywood stardom, only to realize later she was out of work and had been blackballed all over town. He would lure the tender child into his web in order to fully complete his plan.

"I am such a genius," he pronounced.

"Yes, sir. You are, sir," said Sidney, sitting nearby. Acknowledging Von Heller with a sickening smile.

Von Heller, glancing over at Sidney, squinted his puffy, bespectacled eyes. He thought the little man was almost too much of a simpering yes-man even for him, but who else could he find so efficient and lacking any trace of a conscience. He knew his secretary would do as he asked without question and that was all that mattered to a man like Bruno Von Heller; a creature who enjoyed breaking people down and watching them squirm in the dirt.

The two of them remained in the privacy of Von Heller's warren the remainder of the day, carefully going over all the details of his latest production and evil plans against Alexis Moxley, and others. They had the misfortune to find themselves on Bruno's list. Bruno had made special arrangements for this young starlet.

Reginald looked up expectantly from the paper he was reading, removing a pair of small glasses from his face, when he heard the sound of the Ford's motor. Dominic, oily shop rag in hand, stepped out of the garage as the car approached, but vanished into the shadows again once he was sure it was Alexis coming up the drive. Pedro, having finished his work, went home for the day.

She roared into the driveway so quickly Reginald thought she was going to hit the garage. "Surely she doesn't drive that fast all the time?"

The girl was out of the car almost before it stopped rolling. She had to run back to set the brake. He could tell, by her agitated state, something was not right. He walked over to meet her on the driveway.

"How did it go? Is everything all right?" he asked seriously.

"Everything is just wonderful."

He had never seen her smile this much, a sure indication something was amiss, but her mood was contagious and he grinned.

"What happened?"

"Oh, you'll never guess." Before he could say anything she told him excitedly about getting the role in Von Heller's new film.

"This is proceeding according to plan, my girl. Let's go in and celebrate."

"I need a drink to calm my nerves. I have never been this excited in my life Reggie.
I can't wait to tell you all about it."

"And I can't wait to hear all about it," he said.

The house felt cool as they crossed the stones of the entryway. Reginald went over to the bar as Alexis kicked off her shoes and flopped into a soft leather chair, letting out a large sigh of relief. When he turned around, with the drinks in his hands, she was pacing the room.

"Here. It looks like you need this," he handed her a glass and sat down.

"I actually got a big part in Von Heller's new movie. Can you believe it?"

"Did he recognize you?"

"Yes, he was really very polite."

"Von Heller polite? That is difficult to envision."

"Well, he was very nice about everything. I never expected it. I was so scared. I read for a small role in the film and he said he liked my work and wanted me to read for another part. I auditioned for the bigger part and he actually clapped. Can you believe it Reggie?"

She was talking very fast now and Reginald had trouble keeping up with her as she moved around the room excitedly. He was beginning to feel agitated by the girl's unbridled emotions.

"Alexis. Please sit down and look at me," he spoke in a calm clear tone. She finally obeyed his request. After several more tries he was able to train his eyes on her's.

"Relax and tell me what happened after you read the part."

"Okay. I'm relaxed now." Her enthusiasm had subsided somewhat for now.

"Did Von Heller make mention of me?"

"No," her voice was oddly quiet.

"Did he say anything about your sister?"

"Lillian?"

"Yes, did Von Heller bring her name up?"

"No."

"What part did you read for?"

"The leading female role. It's a horror film." She was speaking in a monotone now.

"Why do you think he gave you the part?"

"Because he could see I have talent."

Reginald did not doubt the girl possessed some ability, but he seriously doubted Von Heller would give such an important role to an untried actress; especially one associated to an enemy. Von Heller didn't operate that way and this made Reginald suspicious of his motives. Reginald thought Bruno would humiliate the girl and send her packing. He certainly never expected she would be offered a leading role in the film. Von Heller was up to no good and Reginald knew it could only lead to Alexis getting hurt in some way. He also knew Von Heller would think nothing of using the girl to get even with him. This madness had to be stopped at once, before she was drawn into the web.

"Alexis, this is too dangerous to continue. You must not go back to that studio."

As his words sank into her consciousness she became fully aware and her eyes flew open.

"What do you mean Reggie?"

"I mean what I said Alexis. Von Heller is an evil

man and very possibly the one who is responsible for your sister's death. He would not have been so good to you unless he has a plan to get to you, or me, in some way."

"I finally have a chance to make it big in the movies Reggie. This may be the only way for me to become a star."

"Nonsense. If you truly have real talent you can make it in the movies, eventually."

"Eventually? That could be a lifetime."

"Alexis. Von Heller is up to something and you know it. He is trying to draw us in."

"You don't know that for sure Reggie. I need to keep going so that we can find out if Von Heller is the one behind the murders."

"You want to be the bait for a murderer? Do you know what you are playing at girl?"

"At least I can try to find something out about Von Heller and maybe get my career started too."

"I still say it is too dangerous." Now Reginald paced the room.

"Reggie this may be our only chance to find something that we can make the police believe. I don't want to get killed, but I'm willing to take my chances."

"Is there any way I can change your mind?"

"No. And don't try to mesmerize me again."

"I was not trying to mesmerize you. I was trying to get you to relax."

"You know you can't stop me Reggie. My mind is made up."

"All right. If you think you must go ahead with this folly, than do as you please, but I must be honest with you about those horror films," he said with a lopsided grin. "They are not a great way to advance your career."

That evening, after dinner, they had decided to retire to the small study in order to discuss what they knew about the case. Reginald poured his best cognac into crystal glasses and the two actors sat in the comfortable leather chairs. They would be moving Alexis into her apartment tomorrow and Reginald thought he would attempt to dissuade the girl one last time.

"You know you will be completely on your own Alexis. I will not be around to help you if something occurs."

"I realize that, I also understand the danger I could be in if Von Heller is the one trying to cover up his crimes. He would stop at nothing to keep us from finding out the truth," she said.

"Right. I'm glad you know the danger and now perhaps I can change your mind about moving out."

"It wasn't so many days ago you were trying to talk me out of moving in with you Reggie. Could it be that you are going to miss my company?"

"No. I still find you completely annoying, but you must not put yourself in an already dangerous situation."

"Thanks for your concern, but you know we decided I must move out in order for it to appear convincing. Von Heller will have me observed, no doubt."

"No doubt. But is all of this really so important to you that you would risk your career or your life?" he asked.

"Do you really need to ask me to know the answer Reggie?"

"No. I suppose not, my girl. You are hard-headed as well as annoying."

Reginald refilled their glasses with the expensive liquor. He ran out of arguments for keeping the actress in the safety of his home and he knew any further attempts on his part would only increase her resolve. Alexis was young and beautiful and she had an unbeatable spirit about her that would undoubtedly lead to her success.

He felt an odd mixture of emotions when he imagined his home without the girl and wondered if the blackness would return to his soul when she had gone, or if he would find solace in alcohol once more. He thought of sharing these concerns with her, but his pride would not allow it.

"Who will do my cooking when you are gone Alexis?"

"I've made arrangements with Pedro's wife, Maria, to step in as your cook until Grace is able to return to work."

"Oh, yes. Maria is a fine cook as well as a good housemaid. Thank you."

"You know I won't be able to visit you for a while, don't you Reggie?"

"I know that."

"Will you be okay?"

"Of course. I have much to do. I must finish my play and I need to make inquiries in Barstow concerning the whereabouts of Joe Fisk."

"We still need to meet somewhere private in order to discuss our latest findings. Do you have any ideas?"

"We sound like lovers who are married to other people."

"Yes, it does seem that way, doesn't it?" she laughed nervously.

"We could always meet at my private booth at the diner. I could even arrange a more private place with the owner."

"That sounds okay. How will we plan our meetings? Do you think it will be safe to talk over the phone?"

"I think it will be all right, but we should probably meet at a prearranged time just to be on the safe side. We can plan this in more detail at a later date."

"This really does sound a lot like two people doing something naughty," she giggled.

He attempted to change the subject. "It stands to reason that Von Heller did it."

"He certainly had the motive if you were the one who killed his brother."

"He had the opportunity and method to commit the murders too. I think your number one goal is to strike up a conversation with him about his past. Try to find out where Von Heller is from and get the man to talk about his brother. Push him as much as you can, but remember to talk as calm and soothing as possible. If you can get him to relax his guard, perhaps he will reveal some information about himself."

"I wish you could be with me Reggie. You know so much about this stuff and I will be going in untried."

"Yes. You will be flying blind, but remember how you got through all those tough times alone when your father was sick. You got through it and you will this too."

At the mention of her father and the painful memories, her eyes became moist and her hand shook a little as she reached up to wipe them.

"I'll do whatever it takes to find the one who killed my sister and ruined your career."

"To hell with my career. I just want the bastard who took Lillian away from us brought to justice."

Now she could see that his eyes were wet with grief and she knew she must find a way to make Von Heller admit his guilt. She would do this for them and for her dead sister who could not speak for herself.

Chapter 14.

One week after she moved out of Reginald's house and began her film career, Alexis drove herself to the diner to discuss any new developments concerning the case, as they now referred to it. They met in the private booth in a corner of the place; it sat somewhat away from other's eyes and ears.

Irving Berlin's lyrics crooned from the radio," just around the corner, there's a rainbow in the sky, so let's have another cup of coffee, and let's have another piece of pie."

"As long as we keep our voices down I don't think we will be overheard. Have you managed to get close enough to Von Heller to talk to him?" Reginald asked.

"I've been trying all week, but I'm so busy. I don't want to do anything that will seem too suspicious," she replied.

"How is the film going?"

"It's a grueling schedule. We work ten or twelve hours every day of the week. I called you as soon as I could get a break. Bruno is a slave driver."

"Is he still being kind or have you seen his evil side yet?" Reginald asked.

"He's been very considerate to me, but I've seen how he treats other people and it turns my stomach. I can't wait until we're finished with this film."

"How much longer do you think it will be before the movie is completed?"

"Von Heller wants it finished in two weeks. I don't mind hard work, but I really had no idea actors worked like this."

Reginald thought the girl looked thinner than usual and when the food arrived she wasted no time before digging in. How different she was from her sister, who would not have stepped foot in a place like this, he thought.

"Are you taking care of yourself Alexis?" he asked with concern.

"We don't get many breaks and I get home so late I

usually just go straight to bed. I eat whenever I get a chance."

"Yes, I remember those days myself, only it was in an airplane at a thousand feet above the ground. They crank out those movies to an entertainment starved public every two or three weeks."

"I suppose it makes it worthwhile to think people will be able to take their minds off day to day worries and enjoy the film. I still can't believe I'm actually starring in a Hollywood movie."

"How do you like your part?" Reginald asked.

"I'm really getting into character with this role. It's about an evil professor who becomes enamored with a *young* girl and he has his trained gorilla kidnap her."

"A trained ape?"

"Well, it's not a real gorilla. A guy in a monkey suit carries me around and I scream a lot." She was blushing now.

"Sounds fascinating," Reginald snickered into his palm.

"Stop laughing at me Reggie." She kicked him in the knee.

"Ouch. Stop kicking me. I suppose a girl has to start somewhere these days. At least its not one of those desert sheik movies with you running around half nude."

"Those went out a few years ago. Everyone wants to see horror and gangster movies now," she said.

"I should have tried out for the gorilla part," he said dryly.

"I think you would have made a cute monkey," she giggled.

"I could have carried you away to my nest in the trees."

"What would we do in the trees?" she asked mischievously.

"Why, we would pick fleas off of each other. What else?"

He expected the kick, under the table, before it came.

Murder By Plane 143.

Later that day, when she returned home to her quaint apartment in the city, Alexis readied herself for bed. She had returned to the studio after lunch with Reginald and worked through the afternoon and into the evening. She immediately kicked off her shoes upon entering the small bedroom. This was quickly followed by the remainder of her clothes and a long soak in a hot bath with a cool drink in her hand. This had been her routine for a solid week.

Her thoughts returned to the day's events and finally to her meeting with Reginald. He seemed sad and she wondered if it could be something to do with her moving out. It wasn't so much in his words as in his eyes, she thought. She and Reginald had become so close over the last several weeks; the pair had been through so much together. He had been her protector, and provider, during this eventful time in her life and her feelings for him had definitely deepened. She wasn't sure exactly how she felt about Reginald St. John or how he felt about her, but she knew the two of them shared a common bond. She also knew neither one would ever give up trying to find Lillian's killer.

As her mind mulled over these complicated thoughts, her body began to relax in the bath. Suddenly a strange noise came from the other room, the unmistakable sound of a doorknob turning. She was startled; her body tensed.

Alexis quickly sat up in the tub and tried to remember if she had locked the door behind her when she came in this evening. Maybe I'm just being silly and paranoid, she thought. I've never lived alone and it's just getting to me. She heard it again. "Damn!" she whispered, and standing up, grabbed a towel from the rack beside her. Now the doorknob turned this way and that without regard to the noise being made.

Alexis stood at the bathroom door clutching the towel around her and wondering what she should do next. She hurried across the bedroom to the nightstand beside her bed. Her heart felt as though it would beat out of her chest at any minute. Reginald had purchased a small caliber revolver and instructed her on its basic operation. She quickly removed the small pistol from the drawer and moved over to the bed to change into her silk robe. The noise stopped for the moment, but she could still feel the blood pounding in her ears.

Now a new sound came from the front of the apartment, the unmistakable creak of her door opening slowly. There was only one lock on the solid wooden door and this seemed secure enough to satisfy Reginald. Alexis was terrified. She held the gun out with both hands just as Reginald had instructed. Her instincts told her to hide behind something for protection. Maybe confront the intruder and blast away? The revolver felt so small and her hands were shaking uncontrollably. Her entire body felt cold as she advanced to the bedroom door to face the trespasser.

Reginald had decided to continue his nightly surveillances of the girl's apartment in the hope of providing some protection for her. He had been doing this every night since she moved out. This night it had paid to be cautious. He was sitting in the Duesenberg after she had gotten home when he noticed a figure silently creeping up the fire escape.

Reginald quickly made his way into the building, up the stairs to the third floor, to her apartment. After several attempts to turn the knob, on the off-chance she had not locked it, he used his skeleton key to open the door. He peered into the small front room and slowly swung the door open. He did not want to call out to her as the killer could be at one of her windows by now. He wondered where she was.

Had the girl been so exhausted from filming all day that she had gone straight to bed? He moved silently into the dark sitting room, crouching behind a small chair. Only a single small lamp provided illumination for the front room. He could see the bedroom was well lit. She must have been in the bathroom getting ready for bed. What a perfect time for the killer to attack a helpless woman.

He began to experience a sensation of momentary panic at the thought of a murderer slipping a cord around the girl's neck as she innocently sat in her bath, or strangling her in her sleep. Reginald quickly stood up and moved forward to the bedroom door. He slowly crept toward the open bedroom door feeling every cell in his being poised to react. Reginald removed the large revolver from his waistband and held it in a relaxed grip at his side. All his senses were heightened and every muscle remained ready for quick action as he advanced across the floor.

Reginald knew better than to charge into the bedroom unexpectedly. He had been in close combat and had seen the results of rash action being taken by untrained men. That was how innocent people ended up in the morgue. He knew Alexis might have heard his entry and been frightened. She was probably hiding in a closet. Why take any chances if it could mean life or death for either of them. How ironic it would be if he and the girl fatally shot each other while the killer watched from one of the windows. He almost chuckled out loud as the mental picture played out through his mind. This could be made into a movie scene. Perhaps it was time to announce his presence before something really did go wrong.

Alexis covered half of her scantly clad body behind the open bedroom door. The gun held tightly in her upraised arm. She found it difficult to keep her breathing under control. She listened carefully for any new sounds. The barely audible footsteps had stopped, as if the intruder waited just beyond the doorway to the bedroom. Should I say something out loud? That could warn the creep, he would open fire on her, the end of Alexis Moxley, she thought. Hell no, not tonight. No, she would not give up without a fight. Alexis decided to wait as quietly as possible, behind the thin panel, until the killer made his way into her bedroom. Then shoot. She felt perfectly within her rights to take deadly action to defend herself. This is my home, damn it. Her anger increased her resolve and worked to calm her nerves, the hysteria was replaced with an instinct to survive.

A scuffling noise came from her bedroom window which was across the room, behind her. Her panic increased as she glanced in that direction.

Her fears were confirmed as a dark form tried to raise the window. If she turned away from the door, she would be completely vulnerable to the person in her apartment who was probably right outside the bedroom, but if she kept her back to the window she would be attacked from behind. Her body felt so cold she began to shake uncontrollably. The flimsy robe clinging to her damp body did very little to hide her nakedness, adding to her feeling of helplessness. She had to reach deep within herself, through the terror of the moment, to find the strength to fight.

She moved out into the middle of the room, away from the door, so she could face both intruders. Alexis was prepared to fire the pistol. At that instant she heard a male voice whispering her name, out of the darkness of the other room. Reginald stepped into the light just as the bedroom window shattered and Alexis fired the little gun.

"Alexis. Don't shoot. It's me Reginald." He rushed to her side.

She had fired a round into the wall near the window and now trained the pistol on Reginald's midsection. He could see her body trembling and the fright in her eyes.

"Reggie?" she sobbed.

Reginald quickly looked in the direction of the window and saw the broken glass. The intruder was nowhere to be seen.

"I think you scared him away." He inspected the opening.

"That was you opening my door? Why didn't you knock? I might have shot you."

"The thought did occur to me, but I did not want to warn the person on your fire escape."

"I ought to shoot you for scaring the daylights out of me. " She collapsed on the bed with the gun beside her and a small pillow covering some of her exposed body.

"How did you know that someone was sneaking around on my fire escape?"

"Dominic and I have been taking turns watching your neighborhood. I'll have to board up this damaged window tonight."

"What? Why didn't you tell me what you were up to Reggie. I could have killed one of you."

"I thought it best to let you go about your routine without being aware of us," he said.

"But why?"

"I thought someone would make a move eventually and I was right. If you had been overly cautious in your manner, he may have suspected something."

"So you used me as bait to trap a mad killer?"

"Something like that. I am sorry, my girl, but I did not know a better way to achieve my goal of trapping the murderer. It almost worked too."

"Well next time, will you please let me in on the plan. I'm sitting here almost naked and still terrified."

"Yes, I can see that. Perhaps I should go into the other room and get you a stiff drink."

"No Reggie. Don't leave me alone right now. Should we call the police?"

"I don't think we should call the police. They would file a report and that would be the end of it. Remember Gladys Fisk's apartment?"

"Yeah. What makes me think that they would do anything different now?"

"It is only one pane broken out of the window. I will cover it temporarily tonight and have my gardener, Pedro, fix it properly tomorrow."

"Thanks. I guess I'll have that drink now. I think I'm still in shock."

After Reginald returned from the small kitchen with two glasses of bourbon, he sat on the end of the bed nearest to the broken window. He did not tell Alexis how much of her incredible body was revealed to him when he entered the room. He felt somewhat guilty for breaking into her apartment while she was in her bath. Reginald sipped the smooth whiskey and tried to keep his eyes averted as they conversed.

"You know that I can't go home after what has occurred here tonight? Do you want me to return to the car after I fix the window?"

"No, you can't sleep out in the car. You can stay here tonight," she said.

"I'll find something to repair the broken window pane."

"Don't bother. The warm night air feels good and I need another drink."

The next day Reginald went to Max Carver's office to find out if the lawyer had discovered anything important concerning Claire Caldwell or Joe Fisk. He knew Max had many connections around town and could locate almost anyone. Joe Fisk was still the one link that would probably lead them to the killer. Reginald's back ached something fierce from his restless night spent on the small loveseat; his legs hanging over the armrest. He should have gone back to the comfort of the Duesenberg's spacious backseat. Reginald resisted the urge to think about Alexis and her skimpy robe.

"Do you think Mr. Fisk is still in the desert Max?"

"It was impossible to find anyone out there who

could tell me anything useful over the phone Reg. Talk about the boonies," the lawyer said.

"I see what you mean. Should I plan a trip to the Mojave then?"

"It would take weeks to find that old man, my friend. There's no telling where he could be. Why don't you just give it up and go on with your life Reg?"

"You know I can't do that Max. I have to follow this through to the end."

"Yes, I know how you can be with these things Reg."

"What do you mean?"

"I remember how you hammered those Germans into the ground during the war."

"Let's not rehash those dry, old, memories Max," Reginald said flatly.

"My point is that you never gave the rest of us a chance to claim any of the glory Reg. You pursued those enemy planes like a lone wolf out for blood," Carver said.

"Glory? That is a lot of nonsense Max. I was only doing my part in the war. I never enjoyed killing those Germans. Some of them were just boys."

"Like Bruno Von Heller's brother maybe? Oh, come on, Reg. You know it was a thrill to go out alone and find an adversary. Just you, and the enemy, in single combat."

"Maybe it was a thrill for you old friend, but not for me," Reginald replied.

"But at least you got enough kills under your belt to be counted an ace," Carver said.

Chapter 15.
Bruno Von Heller enjoyed nothing more than making others feel small in his presence. He sat just off the sound stage of his newest production and continued to micro-manage the cast and crew, as if he were the only person capable of making a good decision. This resulted in many extra and unnecessary takes during the filming. The actors and stage crew were exhausted before the day's shooting was half completed. Nerves were constantly on edge and tempers flared. One seasoned actor had already walked off in anger and another one fired.

Alexis had no idea being an actress could be so stressful. She was beginning to have second thoughts about the entire idea. I finally get a major role in a Hollywood movie, she thought, and it's on a set run by a madman; possibly the one who murdered my sister. Alexis had seen Von Heller at his worst now and it was not a pretty sight, thankfully, he never directed it at her. She thought it strange he behaved decently toward her while he treated everyone else as if they were beneath him. Clearly the man was unbalanced.

The day's work continued steadily, despite the loss of several members of the cast, including the actor in the gorilla suit. Alexis felt tired, beyond exhaustion, after a ten hour day on the set and only a few hours sleep the night before. Relieved, she could finally stagger off the set and find her way to her small dressing room located down a long narrow hallway. Alexis smiled when remembering the look on Reginald's face when she asked him to stay the night. As she approached the dressing room, the door was open. A feeling of panic swept over her as she stepped into the small room.

Bruno Von Heller's bulk sat in a small chair near her makeup table.

"You did fine work today young lady," his smile was sleazy.

Murder By Plane 151.

At that same moment Reginald was thinking about Alexis as he sat behind his antique rolltop desk in the study. A crystal snifter sat close at hand, half-filled with his best brandy. He had been at the typewriter working on his play, off and on, throughout the day. Earlier he had received a call from Sergeant Atkins. The sergeant told Reginald the police were still pouring over evidence found at the scene of Brogan's death and they hoped to find fresh leads very soon, but no new leads had been found thus far.

Try as he might, Reginald could not push the image of Alexis, standing in the middle of the bedroom, out of his mind. When he had entered the room she looked almost a heroic figure with the wet robe plastered to her beautiful nude body, the pistol in her hand, and a fierce determined look on her face. The mental picture and the feelings it stirred inside him would not leave him alone. He was glad he had kept watch over her, but it seemed apparent the girl was capable of taking care of herself now.

He leaned back, took a small sip of brandy and tried to make sense of the puzzle surrounding the murders. Why had Lillian been killed? What about the others that had died? Where was the real proof of murder? Perhaps this whole thing was a series of accidents? The old emotions, having waited quietly in the wings like phantoms, began to reemerge onto the stage of his mind. Reginald fought the feelings of guilt, depression and self-loathing which returned when Alexis moved out.

He now realized he had come to depend on her for emotional support. But what if the murderer was real and Frank Brogan's death was no accident? What if the fire at the Studio, that same night, was deliberately set. What about the destruction of Gladys Fisk's apartment and the attempted break in last night? He had found a clue at the scene of Don Denison's death. A scrap of paper with a blood spot and some numbers on it, the only tangible clue they had so far. A clue, now kept in a

152. T.E.Avery

paper envelope at the bottom of a police storage locker. Those numbers were the same as the first three in the address of Bernie's place; the bar where they had sought the one witness who could identify the murderer. Reginald's mind struggled to solve the riddle, while his emotions fought the shadows trying to invade his being. He tasted the strong liquor again and backed away from the desk.

Reginald knew if he could locate Joe Fisk and force him to talk about what he had seen on the night before the Nieuport's crash, it could lead them to the truth. It would mean a road trip across the mountains to the Mojave Desert and a search for someone who did not want to be found, or so it seemed.

How could he think about leaving at a time when Alexis was under the control of Bruno Von Heller? No, he could not leave at the present time. Fisk would have to wait. He and Max Carver would continue to try to locate Mr. Fisk by telephone or until they contacted someone who had seen the old man. For that matter, how could he even be certain Fisk was really in the desert? Reginald rubbed his weary eyes and took a deep breath. His thoughts returned to Alexis and he wondered how she was getting along. He questioned himself. Perhaps I should call her and talk for a few minutes.

They could have supper together at the diner again and discuss the facts of the case and her work at the Studio. He wondered if she had made any progress with Von Heller.

Reginald had seen Bruno dispose of young actors before and the man was certainly out to devour Alexis. He knew how these things usually went, but they had to find out if Von Heller was the murderer. How would the girl get close enough to the monster without being destroyed?

Alexis felt her neck muscles stiffen as she entered the small dressing room.

"Mr. Von Heller. Why are you in my dressing room?" she asked in surprise.

"Please, just call me Bruno. I wanted to compliment you on your work. You are a very talented young woman and I think you will go far in the movies, Miss Moxley."

Alexis looked at the person sitting before her and fought every survival instinct in her being. She wanted to run out the door as fast as her feet could carry her and at the same time grab something, heavy or sharp. This could be the man who was responsible for taking her sister's life. Every cell in her body wanted to take some kind of violent action against this evil creature, but she knew that this could be her one chance to get close enough to find the truth. She stepped over to the other chair and sat down near Von Heller.

"You can call me Alexis," she smiled nervously.

"Alexis. Such a nice name for such a lovely young thing." He took her small hand in his own doughy paw and gazed at her with his diminutive pig eyes. He could not keep his eyes from traveling the length of her body. She felt queasy.

"Thank you Bruno. I really do appreciate the opportunity you have given me. I never dreamed that I would be in a movie after only a few months in Hollywood." She forced herself to smile again, trying to keep from getting sick. "I don't know how I'll ever repay you for your kindness."

He squeezed her hand and stared at her breasts. "Oh, I will think of something, my dear." She felt bile rising in the back of her throat.

He noticed the look of alarm on her face and made an ugly sound that might have been a laugh. "I was thinking of asking you to accompany me to a new club to hear the Dorsey brothers. You have been working hard on this film, as have I, and we need to relax a little. We will have a fine dinner and listen to the orchestra. It will be a grand time. Just the two of us." He kissed her hand.

Alexis felt as though she were on the edge of an abyss ready to plunge into its depths. She knew that if she refused him it would be the end of her career at this studio and maybe at any film studio in Hollywood. If she accepted it would mean getting closer to the repulsive creature. It was not as if he were asking anyway.

Alexis could see by his smile of false confidence he had made up his mind. She knew what she had to do.

"Thank you Bruno. That sounds wonderful."

"We will go tomorrow night at seven o'clock. You will be ready, yes?" He rubbed his fat hands together.

"Yes, and thank you." She forced another smiled.

"I will go now and allow you to change your clothes." He stood, smiled and waddled to the door.

Alexis watched as he made his way out of the room and turned to glance at her once again. His expression became serious and his voice deepened.

"You look very tired this evening. Perhaps you did not get enough sleep last night. Go home and get some rest young lady and you must make sure that you secure your apartment too. I do not want anything to happen to my best actresses."

As soon as the door closed Alexis grabbed a small waste basket near her dressing table and emptied her stomach.

"How could Von Heller have known about the attempted break-in at your apartment last night unless he had something to do with it?" Reginald asked.

Reginald and Alexis had again decided to meet at the little, out of the way, diner not far from his home. The place was not as busy at this hour, but the radio still blasted the big band Jazz from the opposite side of the room.

Reginald didn't know how the owner always made sure they got the same private booth in the corner, but he was glad for the seclusion. They knew Von Heller kept close watch over his people and his security men would surely be following her. Their only hope was that Alexis, in the Ford Roadster, had out-driven the Studio stoolies again. Any chance they now had of finding Von Heller's connection to the murders would surely be dashed by him finding out the two had been meeting for dinner at least once a week.

"It had to have been one of his hired thugs Reggie." She took a small bite of her food.

"You don't seem as hungry as you usually are. Are you feeling all right?"

"Yeah. It's just that I'm still a little queasy after my encounter with Von Heller."

"The creep had some nerve letting himself into your dressing room. What do you suppose his motives were?"

"I don't know. I opened the door and there he was. At least we know that it couldn't have been him on the fire escape last night."

"Yes, he is too fat. He would never be able to get around like that. Whoever it was, definitely moved fast."

"I saw him up close and personal this evening and his only fast moves were on me."

"You mean he made advances toward you?" His voice increased in volume.

"More like insinuations really. And he did ask me out, of course."

"Did he put his hands on you in any way?"

"He just held my hand and kissed it before leaving."

"Perhaps you should call the whole thing off Alexis. If he is getting that close already it will not be long before he attempts to control you. That is usually the way it goes. He picks out one young starlet and takes complete control over her every move. I don't know what his real motive is, but it always ends up badly for the actress."

"How many girls has he done this to?"

"Several. One of them even committed suicide. I'm telling you Alexis, this is dangerous. You must not allow Von Heller to get too close to you. Your career and your life could be in peril," Reginald warned.

"I can take care of myself Reggie. I won't give this up now. I might be able to gain his trust and get him talking. I need to find out what's going on inside his twisted mind."

"No. You can't do this. If you get that close to him and he finds out what you are up to it could turn out very bad for you."

"I'm going to find out if Von Heller is responsible for the accident that killed my sister and ruined your career."

"At what cost, my girl?"

"I don't care. I'm going to go to the club with him tomorrow night and get him drunk, if I can. That should loosen his tongue."

"You are going to be with a drunken psychopath? This is not a smart move. I am asking you to consider the danger." He placed his hand over hers.

"I'm not that stupid. I know it's dangerous and I'm willing to take my chances." She pulled her hand away.

"I have never said that you were stupid, but you are obstinate. You will not listen to reason."

He could see the anger flash in her eyes now.

"So now you think I'm thick headed?"

"I am not calling you names Alexis. I am only trying to look out for your safety."

"We could sit here all day and argue, but it won't change anything Reggie. If Von Heller is the murderer than we need to prove it. We can't find the one witness that will tell us who was at the hanger that night. This is the only way we have of getting to the truth."

"I am still attempting to locate Fisk. I have got Max on it now," Reginald said. "If anyone can find him that shyster can."

"I hope you're right, but I'm still going out with Von Heller tomorrow night."

"I will be at the club too," Reginald said.

Murder By Plane 157.

"You can't. What if he sees you?"

"I will be out of sight and you will never even know of my presence."

"Okay, but don't mess up my chances with Bruno."

"Bruno? So you are on a first name basis with the scum?"

"Yes. He told me to call him Bruno," she smiled. "What do you think of that?"

"It means that he is moving closer to you for certain. Not too many of his people are allowed to address him in such a casual manner."

"Maybe he genuinely likes me," she smiled again.

"Perhaps he genuinely likes you so much that he wants to devour you like a wolf wants to gulp down a tasty lamb," he added.

"Baa." she tried to make it sound comical, but did not succeed. "Now I am scared."

As the sun began to set and the eastern sky darkened, Claire Cauldwell sat alone in her car watching the two actors inside the diner having an obviously, serious conversation. She had been so sure that Lillian Livingston was dead, but now she could see her talking to Reginald. How could this be happening to her all over again? Claire had worked so hard to become a Hollywood star. She and her father had moved here from Brooklyn after she won a beauty contest at the age of fifteen. Her father said, "She was the prettiest girl in the world and would be the biggest star in the movies." She had done anything, and everything, a girl could do to get into the studios. At first, everything was going her way.

She first saw Reginald St. John on the big screen and fell in love with him immediately. She knew fate would bring them together, somehow, and it had. She could not believe her luck when she had been selected to be his costar in a silent film.

158. T.E.Avery

But the talkies had come along that same year and spoiled everything. Claire thought about her disgrace and embarrassment on the set of her first talking picture with Reginald. The way she had lost her temper and walked away, thinking surely the director would send for her; but he never did. Lillian Livingston was younger and had so much talent, beauty and charisma. Reginald was smitten with her from the first time they met. Claire's eyes burned as she thought about the girl coming along and stealing the love of her life. Now Lillian had come back from the dead to try, once more, to take Reginald away. Claire could not allow that to happen to her again.

She clenched her fists and stared at the illuminated windows of the small diner. What could they be talking about? Claire was sure they must be discussing a plan to destroy her life. That witch had seduced Reginald and turned him against the one woman who had truly shown love and loyalty to him. Claire thought the creature was gone for good, but now she could plainly see the seductress plotting her evil scheme. *Reginald St. John is mine and I will do anything to keep him. Who would blame me for doing what I had to do?*

Chapter 16.

It was another long day of filming on the set of the horror movie and Alexis felt as though she were ready to crumble. She was required to stay in costume all day and her feet were throbbing from having to wear the high heeled shoes that went with the part. Now she had to get dressed to go out with Bruno when all she wanted to do was soak in a hot bath and go straight to bed. Just the thought of Bruno looking at her made her feel violated and dirty. It was a relief he had not been waiting in her dressing room this evening.

She sat on the edge of her small bed and looked over at the new window Reginald had installed yesterday; a strong grillwork and a heavy lock. A curtain of thick fabric shielded her from any prying eyes. The locks on the other windows and outer door had also been changed, making her feel much safer. He wanted to hire a live-in maid to watch over her, but she had refused. Reginald could be almost too thoughtful and protective toward her, yet he seemed distant at other times. There was no denying the strong bond that now existed between them, but she knew their feelings for each other were mixed. Sometimes her feelings for him were more like they would be toward a big brother and at other times she imagined them as lovers. Her thoughts returned to the other night when she had asked him to stay. She had been surprised as the words came out of her mouth before she had really given it any consideration, but she had not regretted asking.

Her body felt battered and bruised from a solid week of being carried around by an actor in a gorilla costume. Bruno refused to use a stunt double for her role in the film and Alexis was beginning to wonder if this was part of his plan to destroy her. What if the guy in the ape suit threw her down a flight of stairs or something? Her imagination began to go into high gear and she felt the fear building inside. She knew Bruno was up to something and she didn't have much time to find out how he was involved in the murders. This had to be the night she would get the information out of him, somehow. Reginald said he would be at the club tonight and this made her feel better, but now she was having doubts.

Bruno would be here in his big black limo in an hour and she would be required to sit next to him all the way to the club. What if he tries something when he has me alone in the backseat? The thought of it made her feel sick as she bent over to pull her silk stockings over her knees. Maybe she should bring the small pistol with her. She could conceal it in her handbag and no one would be any wiser. She reached over to the drawer of the nightstand and pulled it open. The shiny gun seemed more like a toy than a deadly weapon, but she knew it could be her only protection if she were cornered by the killer. The weight of the loaded pistol felt reassuring in her hand. She jammed it into the bottom of her purse and returned to her task of preparing for the evening's events.

From the street below her apartment the watcher could see the girl moving around in her bedroom. Trying to get into the place was useless now that the windows and doors had been secured, beside the fact that she was armed with a gun. Getting close enough to do what had to be done presented a problem that would have to be figured out as the evening proceeded. It was a problem that every predator must deal with from time to time. It looked as though the young actress was definitely going out tonight.

She would need to be followed. Surely she would be alone at some point during the night and that is when she would meet her end. Making her death appear as an accident would be the real challenge.

Murder By Plane 161.

The Dorsey brothers opened the club several weeks ago to the delight of many fans of their Dixieland jazz music. Tommy, the younger brother, was content to play his instrument while Jimmy ran the place. The brothers were known to argue for as long as anyone who knew them remembered, but the present arrangement seemed to work out satisfactorily, at least for the time being, as the place was filled with customers.

Reginald had not been overly fond of Jazz music, but recently listened to it for research for his play. He had grown up, during the pre-war years, listening to classical music and show tunes. Now he found that, at times, he could actually enjoy the hot new jazz sound. Perhaps it was not only for the very young after all. He sat at a table near the entrance to the club. Reginald wore heavy black framed glasses and a fake bushy mustache. He had also combed his hair differently as part of the disguise. No one recognized the movie star tonight as he leaned back in his chair casually scanning the crowd in the large, smoke filled, room. At least no one had approached him to request an autograph.

He arrived early in order to procure a table near the front door. This would allow him to observe everyone who entered. The weight of the French revolver in his dark blue, double breasted, jacket gave him some assurance. His light brown fedora sat on the table at his elbow, a glass of Scotch whisky remained in front of him untouched. He had ordered the drink, but knew he must remain fully alert for tonight's business. Dominic remained close at hand with the Duesenberg, just in case he would be needed. Reginald was taking no chances tonight.

A hush fell over the place as young Glenn Miller began to play a couple of practice solos on his trombone. Reginald could not help but tap his foot during Miller's act. No, this music is for the young at heart everywhere, he thought. He wished Alexis was by his side right now and not in the clutches of Von Heller. He had no doubt she would be enjoying this music. A cigarette girl, in a skirt revealing well turned calves, carried a tray of assorted smokes to his table.

"Cigarette, cigar?"

"No thank you."

"Are you sure sir?"

Reginald thought of himself holding a large cigar with his bushy mustache and glasses and chuckled at the image. He could pass for Groucho Marx in this costume.

The girl smiled with him, but did not get the joke.

"No thank you," he repeated.

"Okay sir. If you say so."

He tried to relax and listen to the orchestra while discreetly watching the crowd coming through the door. It was a group consisting mostly of younger twenty-somethings. Boys and girls, in small gaggles of friends, were looking for a good time to distract themselves from their day to day concerns. These kids were too young to have been a part of the Great War, Reginald mused. Not part of his lost generation.

Of course, there would be other wars to fight now that this Hitler fellow had taken control in Germany. He felt this country was fighting for it's life with the depression. Five million out of work and growing.

He hoped Roosevelt knew what he was doing and could turn this economy around. Reginald knew he would never have to worry about money, but what about regular working people? All the glitter of Hollywood, and the clubs, and the booze and the cigarettes, could not hide the fact that so many families were in need. As the troublesome thoughts ran through his mind, he spotted Alexis moving past him followed closely by Bruno Von Heller. He could see Bruno's fat hand on the lower part of her back. He knew this was going to be a very long night and wished that he and the girl were back at his seaside house.

Murder By Plane 163.

They were directed to a table across the room and not far from the band. Von Heller seemed so out of place here and Reginald thought the fat man had done his research well. Alexis loved the big band jazz sound. She had been constantly changing the radio channels at home, and in the car, searching for live jazz music.

This was one reason Reginald had decided to write the music into his play. He felt it possessed an energy and originality which would add something to his work. He realized how much he missed having the girl around with her youthful, effervescent ways. Surely these young people would find their way out of these troubled times and win wars.

Alexis could feel the pig eyes of Bruno drilling into her back as he almost pushed her across the floor, to a reserved table near the dance floor. She nearly giggled out loud when Bruno cringed as a trumpet blasted him before he sat down. The short, heavy, man was completely out of his element here and she wondered why he had chosen to bring her to the club. If anyone deserved an all night headache, he did, she thought. She tried not to notice

Bruno staring across the table almost willing her to meet his gaze. Talking was impossible with the band playing, so she mustered a smile to appease him. He reached across the tiny table and took her hand in his sweaty fingers. Alexis fought the urge to pull away.

She wondered if Reginald had made it to the club as he said he would. She pretended to show interest in Von Heller while carefully looking around the huge room. Bruno selected a big cigar from the tray being offered by a cigarette girl wearing a white blouse and short skirt. Alexis was distracted by the orchestra when the girl came around the table to offer her a cigarette. Alexis did a double take when she looked up because it appeared the woman was sneering at her. Maybe my exhaustion is playing tricks with my mind. The woman turned away before Alexis could be certain if she had, indeed, been studying her with a hateful gaze.

"I don't smoke anyway so just go ahead and walk away," she said with annoyance.

"Did you say something my dear?" Bruno had to shout to be heard.

"No. I was talking to myself Bruno. I'm just a little tired tonight."

"What? Speak up my dear. This music is so loud." He squeezed her hand too hard.

"Excuse me Bruno; I need to go to the powder room." She felt that if she didn't get away soon she would scream.

"What? What did you say?"

"I said I have to go to the ladies room."

"What?" Bruno yelled.

Alexis stood up and leaned across the small table.

"I have to go to the girl's room." The music stopped just before she yelled the words at the top of her lungs. Laughter could be heard throughout the room and she felt like getting under the table, but just stood looking around like a cornered deer.

"Oh." Bruno replied with surprise.

She rolled her eyes and scurried away feeling like a complete idiot.

As she made her way to the ladies room she happened to notice a strange, but curiously familiar, man sitting alone at a small table. He wore thick black framed glasses and had a bushy mustache. She did not pause to consider who it might be, but continued on her way to the women's restroom, weaving through the tables and chairs full of customers.

When Alexis finally made it into the powder room she stood for a minute to catch her breath. The room reeked with the odor of stale cigarette smoke. This night was not turning out to be very enjoyable at all, she thought. The only other person in the room was the surly cigarette girl, in her skimpy uniform, over by the sink. She did not look around as Alexis entered the area occupied by several basins and a small chaise lounge. Alexis sat down, but did not try to converse with the young woman, hoping she would leave soon. There was something strange about her, but she could not decide what it could be.

Alexis decided to seek a moment of solitude by going into one of the stalls with the wooden partitions and latching door. It had been an incredibly long day of working in the tense environment of the sound stage and dealing with Bruno. Now she must associate with the creep on her own time too. But how could she find out any pertinent information from the man unless she spent time with him?

As her mind sifted through these complicated thoughts and emotions her eyes became heavy. She was at the point of drifting into a light doze when she heard the lock on the bathroom door slide into place with a sharp click.

Reginald had been sitting and watching Alexis and Von Heller from his vantage point across the room. He congratulated himself on his forethought in getting to the club early. Now it was up to Alexis to achieve her goal in getting the fat man to loosen up and talk about himself. Perhaps this had not been such a bad idea after all, he thought. Alexis seemed to know what she was doing and together they could bring the killer to justice and all of this mess to a close. He thought about what it would mean to him to find out he had not been the cause of his fiancée's death. Would he feel as if an enormous weight had been lifted from his shoulders after a long year of guilt and self-loathing? He hoped it could be that way.

He was lost in his thoughts when the cigarette girl brushed past him trailing her hand across his arm. He was shaken from his reverie by her provocative body language as she walked past. He followed her with his gaze. The girl turned her head around to glance at him over her bare shoulder, but continued her path to the ladies room.

She seemed vaguely familiar to him. He was racking his mind when the music stopped. There was a commotion and the sound of laughter. He looked around just as Alexis was making her way toward his table. Von Heller was still sitting awkwardly at the small table like a chubby, porcine statue. Reginald tried, as discreetly as possible, to meet her eyes as she walked by his table, but it was obvious that she could not see through his disguise. He thought it bizarre how easy it was to hide behind a simple mask. It was at that moment the truth came flooding into his memory, the truth about someone else in disguise, here, tonight.

Inside the bathroom stall Alexis strained her ears for any further sounds coming from outside. She almost decided the strange cigarette girl had departed the bathroom and she had been mistaken about the noise coming from the door. Suddenly a loud bang on the stall door made her jump. This was going too far, she thought angrily.

"Who's there?" her voice sounded small.

The next bang on the door made her jump again, her hands began shaking.

"Who are you? Why are you doing this?"

"It's me." It was a woman's whispered voice.

"Who is it?"

Another long pause, then the sound of finger nails scraping down the wooden door of the stall. Alexis tried to look under the space beneath the door, but could not get low enough without actually squatting on the floor, and she did not want to be in a vulnerable position now.

"It's me Lillian," the voice was louder now.

"Who is this? Alexis said sharply.

"Why did you come back Lillian?"

"I'm not Lillian. Just go away and leave me alone."

Murder By Plane 167.

"You can't have him Lillian. You have to die again. Why did you come back?"

"You are crazy."

"Reginald and I are in love and no one can ever come between us again. You have to go away. Go back to your grave Lillian."

"Wait a minute. Are you Claire?"

Small noises were coming from the right. Claire had moved into the other stall. This could be her chance to escape, bolting through the stall door and making for the locked bathroom door. Alexis felt the small revolver, through the cloth of her purse, on her lap. This made her feel a little more confident, although she did not relish the idea of using the gun.

"Claire?"

"They called me the "Girl Star" of Hollywood."

"Claire. I'm not Lillian Livingston."

"Don't try to fool me Lillian. You tricked everyone else, but you can't fool me. I was the biggest star. Daddy said I was."

"Claire, you have to listen …."

"Daddy said that I was the prettiest girl in the world. I made it in the movies. I was the biggest star in Hollywood."

"Yes, you were Claire. You still are," Alexis decided to try a different tact with the disturbed woman.

"Yes, I'm the star. I'm the one Reginald wants."

"Claire. Listen to me. You need help. I want to help you."

"No. I don't need your help Lillian. I just want you dead again."

Now Alexis heard louder noises. Claire was standing on the toilet. This meant the insane woman would be climbing over the partition any second. It would allow her the time she needed to get out of the stall; but what if Claire had a weapon? The crazed woman could shoot her in the back or stab her with a dagger. Alexis reached into her handbag and retrieved the small pistol.

Chapter 17.

Too much time had elapsed since Alexis had passed by his table and Reginald felt a growing unease with every minute he counted. He knew who that phony cigarette girl was, or thought he did. He observed the table where Von Heller sat alone and looking self-conscious. His enemy was not so self assured without his entourage to back him up. Reginald wondered why the fat man would venture out like this without his retainers around him for security.

He turned back and looked at the door to the women's restroom that was no more than thirty feet away. This predicament certainly had him stumped. How would he handle this? Reginald got to his feet just as the orchestra began to perform again and Mildred Bailey started to sing. He would enjoy listening to the music if not for this awkward situation he now found himself in. Walking over to the door of the ladies powder room, he stood to one side, listening for any sounds coming from within. The loud jazz drowned out any chance for that.

As bad as he hated the idea, he knew his only choice was to walk into the women's lounge. Everyone was turned toward the stage so he would not be noticed. Reginald braced himself, took a deep breath, and swallowed hard. This would be going against all of his upbringing, but what choice did he have at the moment? What if there was a crazed actress in there with Alexis? He reached for the door knob and was almost relieved when he found it was locked.

"But why would it be locked?" Reginald asked aloud.

Now Reginald knew something was happening in there and just when he had decided to break the door down he heard a loud pop coming from within. It was the unmistakable sound of a small caliber pistol's report, followed by a banshee scream, so loud that people sitting at nearby tables turned and looked his way. The door flung open and the peculiar cigarette girl came crashing out. Her wild, feral eyes looked into Reginald's as she

Murder By Plane 169.

bumped into him, knocking over a table as she ran for the nearest exit. It looked as if her hand was bleeding and indeed he noticed several drops of red on the polished floor.

Reginald quickly recovered from the startling scene and peered into the open door of the ladies room. Again he hesitated, but several customers began to stand up and make their way over to the chaos. He knew that he must act quickly. He walked hastily into the ladies room and seeing no one at the sink area, he investigated the stalls. There was enough space between the closed door of the nearest stall and the floor that he could see Alexis lying on the floor face down. Spots of blood covered the tiles around her. She held the small gun in her hand.

"Alexis?" He called her name in a voice that betrayed his emotions.

He reached under the door and pulled the girl through the space. He could see she was still breathing and had no apparent wounds.

"Thank God, my girl."

He was bending over her and running his hands across her body to check for injuries when several women came into the room to investigate the commotion.

"Hey you. What goes on here?" a young woman called out.

Reginald stood up and scooped Alexis into his arms in one lifting motion. He quickly exited the door; the pistol concealed under her limp body until he was able to stuff it into his waist band.

"Excuse me please. Let me through. My wife has had a dizzy spell."

"Oh. Is that what happened mister?" The girl at the door looked concerned and he could see, by her clothes, that she worked at the club.

"Yes, make way. This happens to her sometimes. I will take her home now."

170. T.E.Avery

"Make way. Get out of the way please." The young woman actually believed his story and the customers were returning to their seats as he was led to a side door. No one asked about the hysterical woman who had ran out earlier. A quick glance over his shoulder revealed Von Heller was not at his table and no where to be seen. The side door took him directly to the parking lot. The girl usher held the door open as he carefully turned sideways to keep Alexis from bumping into the doorframe.

The jazz orchestra continued to play as the door closed and Reginald carried the unconscious girl through the parking lot. Dominic registered a look of surprise and concern on his normally laconic face.

"What happen boss? She okay?"

"I think so. She is breathing anyway. Let's get her home."

Just as Reginald was stepping into the Duesenberg with the girl across his lap, he noticed a fat form moving quickly across the lot and stepping into the back of a black limo. Alexis was beginning to stir as the big car sped away from the club. Her eyes fluttered open and suddenly she was fully awake.

"Reggie? What's happened?"

"I don't know. I thought perhaps you might tell me."

"I'm so tired." Her eyes began to close again.

Reginald looked down at the young woman resting on his thigh.

"We can talk later. You need to take it easy right now, my girl."

"I like it when you call me that," she murmured.

Reginald had been writing his play for several hours after they returned home, when Alexis, wearing a bathrobe and slippers, appeared in the doorway. He had become so involved in the story he had lost track of the time.

"Thanks for putting me to bed again. I guess I was so

Murder By Plane 171.

exhausted from the day's events that I, sort of, collapsed," she said shyly.

"Come in and sit down. Tell me what happened tonight," Reginald pushed away from the desk.

"I think I shot Claire. She was climbing over the bathroom stall divider with a knife."

"You had to defend yourself Alexis. It is good that you had the pistol."

Alexis came into the room and sat down on one of the leather chairs.

"She was like a wild animal. She thought I was Lillian and she wanted to kill me."

"She said that?"

"Yes. Do you think she is the one who has done all of the killing Reggie?"

"She seems to be the obvious choice, but something tells me that there is more to this business."

"I wonder what Bruno did after we left the club?"

"I saw your date deserting the premises in a hurry."

"Why would he leave like that?"

"Perhaps he is involved. The events tonight may have been a setup for all we know."

"Yeah, maybe Bruno is behind it all and Claire is working with him."

"You may be right, my girl. What else did Claire say to you?"

"She said that she wanted Lillian dead so that she could have you all to herself. If that isn't a confession to murder, I don't know what is."

"Yes, so it would appear. We have motive, means and perhaps opportunity. We still do not know that Claire was at the hanger the night before the airplane accident, and how would she know how to sabotage an aircraft?"

"Could she have had help?"

"You mean Don Denison?"

"Yeah. Maybe he helped her and then she got rid of him when we started poking around."

"It is possible, but something still does not quite fit. I am trying to work it out and it keeps eluding me," Reginald said.

"Me too. I think I need a shot of that good brandy of yours after tonight's events. I'm totally wiped out."

"Well, I can't imagine why you would be. You only worked ten hours today with Bruno and then you were attacked by a mad woman."

"She needs help Reggie. You should have seen her face. The poor woman is completely insane."

"She should be institutionalized so she can receive the proper help," he agreed.

"What can we do?" she asked.

"We can only do as we have been and keep working on this case. Are you sure you are still up to it?"

"Of course I am. Do you think I'm going to stop now?" she asked sharply.

"You must be exhausted. Maybe you should go on to bed?" he suggested.

"But I have to be at the Studio at seven in the morning," she said.

"You mean you are still intending to work for Bruno as if nothing had occurred? What if he tries to set you up again?"

"I still need to ask him some questions, aside from the fact that we only have one week left on the film and I have to finish it."

"I hope it will not finish you, my girl."

"I would kick you, but I'm too tired," her speech was slightly slurred from fatigue and the strong drink.

"Then you must go on to bed and I'll have Dominic take you to your apartment in the morning."

"Oh, and what are you going to do tonight?"

"I am going to write for a while and then perhaps I will think about our case into the wee hours."

"What's the play about?"

Murder By Plane 173.

"It is a mystery about a Midwestern girl who comes to Hollywood searching for romance and adventure."

"It sounds exciting." She walked toward the door now.

"Oh, it is. She meets a handsome aviator."

"Does this Midwest girl find romance?" She batted her eyes while leaning against the door.

"I have not gotten that far yet, but I think she has a real chance."

"Well, let me know how it turns out. You know where to find me."

When she left, Reginald found it difficult to concentrate on his work. His eyes drifted toward the doorway where she had just stood.

Reginald was having a pleasant dream, for a change, when he was awakened by the annoying sound of the telephone ringing. He remembered it had been very late when he had finally gone to bed and he had not gotten nearly enough sleep.

"Who would be calling me at this time of the morning?" he asked aloud.

A glance at the bedside clock told him it was only twenty past seven. He realized it could be something important and with a groan he exited the bed and picked up the telephone.

"Hello?"

"Reggie. I've been trying to get through for ten minutes." Alexis' voice was excited, but hushed.

"What has happened?"

"The biplane, it's gone."

"Gone where?" He sounded groggy to her.

"Someone has stolen the studio's Nieuport."

"When do they think it was taken and how? That is a short runway."

"When I got to the studio this morning there were police and studio cops everywhere. Bruno's assistant told me someone had broken into the back lot and flown away in the airplane at dawn.

174. T.E.Avery

I don't know if Bruno has called off filming for today."

"Von Heller has never missed a days work in his career, at least to my knowledge."

"Yeah, its really strange and they say Bruno is no where to be found."

"That is strange indeed, my girl. What else do you know about it?"

"That's pretty much all I can tell you right now. I'm going to try to find out where Bruno can be reached or at least have a long talk with his assistant. I still need to find out more about the fat man."

"Do you need my help? I can be very persuasive at questioning people."

"I've seen both of your methods of questioning Mr. St. John. I think it best, for now, if I try this one solo."

"Be careful Alexis and keep me posted. I will be at home all day."

After disconnecting, Reginald sat on the edge of the bed thinking about what the girl had just told him. His body wanted to return to sleep, but his mind was reeling with questions now. Who could have flown away in the biplane and why? Obviously the Studio had decided the plane was stolen and not just borrowed by a pilot or mechanic or they would not have called the police.

Now the news people would be involved and the next thing you know they would draw his name, and Lillian's, into it. And what about Von Heller? He had been at the club last night, but now he is keeping a low profile for some reason. Reginald was up and pacing the bedroom as the thoughts came flooding into his mind. Nothing seemed to fit together. If Bruno was behind the whole business then why would he do something so obvious. He was a fanatic about everyone showing up on time, every day, and he practiced what he preached.

He hoped Alexis could find Von Heller and clear some things up. Perhaps she would even ask the fat man about his brother and the war. The brother Reginald had

Murder By Plane 175.

killed in a duel over the French countryside sixteen years ago. Reginald tried to push the guilt out of his mind. He and the Nieuport had been a deadly duo during the war, but now it almost seemed the plane, possessing a will of its own, wanted more people to die.

Alexis had arrived several minutes late to work, this morning, worried about Bruno's reaction. The studio was in a state of chaos when she had arrived. Bruno had not been on the set as she had expected and there was talk about an airplane having been stolen. The police and studio security were swarming the backlot all morning.

After her conversation with Reginald, she began talking to some of the other actors and stage hands. Most of them were on their way out the door after finding out shooting had been called off for the day. Everyone, including Alexis, was relieved to have a day of rest. She found a security man standing just outside the stage entrance. The same, rude, guy that had tossed her out when she had been fired from the office, but now he failed to recognize her.

"What's all the commotion this morning?"

"Some nut took off in one of the Studio's airplanes I guess." He tilted his cap back and scratched his scalp. She could see flakes of dandruff falling from his gray hair.

"Oh. I wonder why anyone would want to take an airplane?" she asked.

"I just dunno Miss. Say, don't I know you from somewhere?"

"I'm an actress. You've probably seen one of my films," she lied.

"Oh, yeah. I think I seen you in a couple a movies." He pointed a thick finger.

"Have you seen Mr. Von Heller today?"

176. T.E.Avery

"Nope. He's usually the first one here in the morning, but I didn't see him come in today. I guess he had business elsewhere."

"Thanks. Oh, just one more thing. Did anyone see who took the airplane?"

"One of our guys spotted a man and a woman acting suspicious early this morning."

"What do you mean? What were they doing?"

"Well, they were walking along the fence behind the Studio at five o'clock in the morning, but it was at a distance and he couldn't see their faces. By the time he had gotten over there they had disappeared."

"Well, thanks," Alexis waved.

Now it was time to find Bruno and have a chat with the fat German, she thought. She went back into the main building and along the same hallway she and Reginald had navigated on the night of the fire. She found Von Heller's office and opened the outer door. There was no one working today so she walked into the inner workplace. Von Heller's secretary looked up in surprise when she entered.

"May I be of assistance to you Miss Moxley?" The small man asked curtly.

"Yes, where can I find Bruno. I need to talk to him about something."

"Mr. Von Heller is not at work today," He emphasized the title.

"Okay, but where can I reach him?"

"You can't. He does not want to be disturbed today." He looked over his reading glasses. Now she was getting angry.

"Look, I really need to speak with Bruno today. It's important. Do you understand?"

"If you disturb Brun … ah Mr. Von Heller this morning, we could both be out of work by this afternoon Miss Moxley."

"I won't tell him that you told me that he is at home."

"How did you know he is home?"

"Thanks Sidney." She smiled on her way out.

The phone began ringing by midmorning and continued unceasingly as reporters scrambled to find out more about the missing Studio biplane. Reginald waited to hear from Alexis all morning, but she had not called. He almost decided to go in search of her when Dominic came into the small study.

"Hey Boss. They say on the radio they find a woman's body."

"Who found a woman's body?" Reginald asked in alarm.

"The cops. They find a woman's body up by the Hollywoodland sign."

"Why tell me about it?"

"I thought you should know about it."

"That is unusual and tragic, but I still don't see what it has to do with me."

"A reporter call about the Studio airplane."

"The Nieuport?"

"Yeah boss. The reporter wanted to talk to you about the airplane, but I done like you say. I tell him you not available to talk."

"Thanks Dominic. This day has been filled with many strange events? Has the woman's body been identified?"

"The police don't say boss?"

"Do they know how she died?"

"They not sayin boss. What we gonna do now?"

"We wait Dominic. We wait. That's all we can do at the moment."

Chapter 18.

Bruno Von Heller's mansion in the Hollywood hills was one of those Old World style Italianates. It was set back from the main road behind a low stone wall topped with ornate ironwork. Neatly trimmed hedges and perfectly spaced palms lined the driveway.

Alexis turned onto the cobbled circle drive and parked the roadster in front of the massive double doors. Brick and terracotta tile steps led up to the columned entrance. She wondered how easy it would be for her to gain entry into the movie producer's opulent manor.

An aging English butler answered the door after she rang the bell one time, as if she were expected.

"Yes, Miss?"

"I'm here to see Mr. Von Heller, please."

"I am sorry Miss, but Mr. Von Heller is not receiving guests today. How may I assist you?"

"I would like to talk to Bruno please."

The servant's eyes widened at her obvious lack of manners and her insistence.

"As I told you Miss, Mr. Von Heller is not accepting guests today. If you will relate your business to me I will tell Mr. Von Heller that you called."

"No. I work for Mr. Von Heller and I must speak with him now. This could be a matter of life or death. Do you understand?"

"Yes, Miss. If you will tell me your name and business I will ask Mr.Von Heller if he will receive you."

"My name is Alexis Moxley and I want to talk to him at once."

The butler attempted to close the heavy door behind him, but Alexis pushed her way in quickly.

"I'll just wait in the entry, if you don't mind, Jeeves."

"Jeeves? Well, I never ... I suppose it will have to be all right. Wait here please." He turned away muttering something indiscernible.

Murder By Plane 179.

Alexis sat on a small stone bench in the large and exquisitely decorated entry foyer. The mansion was cool and reminded her of a mausoleum.

Reginald attempted to occupy himself by working on his play, but by lunchtime he began to grow increasingly concerned. He had called the Studio to speak to Alexis, but was told she was not at work today. Upon further inquiry he found that filming had indeed been suspended for the day and the entire cast and crew had left. Now it was nearing one o'clock and he still had not heard from Alexis. His mild concern now turned into worry after he tried, unsuccessfully, to reach her at her apartment.

The telephone rang at one-thirty and Reginald thought Alexis was finally calling to relate that she had been shopping or caught in traffic, but it was the same reporter who had called earlier about the stolen airplane.

"This is Reginald St. John. Why are you calling?" His tone was clipped.

"Yes, Mr. St. John? This is Sam Pensky with the Daily. I'm just calling you, sir, to get your take on the airplane theft at Fairmont Studios. Do you have anything you can tell me about the plane?"

"I do not know anything about a stolen airplane. Why are you calling me about it?" Reginald asked.

"A witness said it was the same aircraft that you used to fly. A biplane from the war, sir. The Studio said the ... let's see ... Nieuport had been reported stolen from the hanger this morning."

"I still do not see what this has to do with me. I am waiting for an important call Mr. Pesky."

"That's Pensky. It was the same biplane you had an accident in a year ago Mr. St. John. The same plane your fiancee' died in, Sir. Now it has been stolen from the Studio you worked for."

Reginald's eyes became unfocused and his ears began to ring at the mention of the accident.

180. T.E.Avery

There was a long pause before he finally spoke.

"Do the police have any leads, sir?"

"No sir, Mr. St. John. The stolen biplane is nowhere to be found. I do think the police are trying to find someone who can identify the pilot though. Do you think it might be someone you know?"

"Of course not. How could it be someone I know?"

"Well, it is your plane and I just thought …."

"It is not my airplane and you need to leave me alone." He slammed the phone down.

Dominic entered the room when Reginald was talking to the reporter.

"What you gonna do now boss?"

"I am not quite sure. Perhaps I should go talk to the police."

"Boss, you don't think …?"

Reginald knew what he was insinuating.

"Do not get carried away Dominic. The dead woman was probably someone we don't know."

"Accident?"

"Yes, an accident," he said quietly, but he knew it wasn't true.

Reginald parked the Duesenberg across the street from the police station and sat for a few minutes before getting out and walking to the main entrance. He dressed casually so he would not draw attention to himself. He pulled the brim of his brown fedora down after spotting several reporters standing at the big front desk, in the station house, talking to a blue clad policeman. He had called around two o'clock and made arrangements to meet with the police concerning the body they found by the Hollywoodland sign.

He avoided the reporters and was taken, by another cop, to a room with a wooden table and two chairs, where he waited on one of the uncomfortable seats. The room smelled of stale cigarettes and sweat.

After Reginald waited for about twenty minutes,

Murder By Plane 181.

Sergeant Atkins came into the room with a younger officer in tow. The older man took a seat across from Reginald while the other policeman stood nearby.

"Hello Mr. St. John. I'm Sergeant Atkins and this is Officer Handley. We talked on the phone earlier, Sir. I think you might remember me from the studio hanger accident."

"Yes Sergeant, I do remember you; however, I do not agree that Don Denison was killed by accident. That is one reason why I came here today."

"Do you have additional information about Mr. Denison's death, Sir?"

"No Sergeant, but surely you cannot believe all of these deaths could have been accidental? What about Frank Brogan's death and the fire at the studio?"

"I see what you mean; and another death associated with that stolen plane. The newspapers are calling it the murder biplane now. I do understand your point Mr. St. John, but there just isn't sufficient evidence to pursue anyone at this time."

"What did you mean another death associated with the airplane?"

"A witness said they saw a woman falling out of the biplane. Since the airplane was identified as the one stolen from Fairmont Studios, it seemed logical to ask someone from there to view the body. They sent one of their personnel secretaries to the morgue and she positively identified the body."

Reginald took a deep breath and asked. "Who was it?"

"Did you know an actress by the name of Claire Cauldwell, Mr. St. John?"

"I knew Claire," Reginald said.

"When was the last time that you saw Miss Cauldwell, sir?"

"Not since I worked on a picture with her several years ago officer," he lied.

"Do you know of anyone who could fly that type of

aircraft sir? I thought those kites were all single seaters."

"There were single seat fighters during the war, but this plane was designed to allow room for a passenger. There are several stunt pilots around town who are capable of flying that airplane Sergeant."

"I see, and you are one of them, aren't you Mr. St. John?"

"I am an adequate enough pilot, but I have not flown an aircraft for a year now."

"How difficult would it be to make a woman fall out of an open cockpit?"

"Not so hard, I imagine, if she wasn't strapped in tightly. The plane could be rolled over in flight to make someone fall out. Any experienced pilot could do it Sergeant."

"I see, and just for the record Sir, where were you at around six o'clock this morning?"

"Am I a suspect Sergeant?"

"Not at this time Mr. St. John, but we may want to ask you more questions at a later date and I'm gonna have to ask you to stay in town for awhile."

"That should not pose a problem as I rarely leave my home Sergeant. That is where I was this morning, as my driver can testify."

"I have something else I need to ask you about, Sir." The sergeant had been holding a plain, brown envelope during the interview. He removed a piece of cloth and spread it on the table. It was a blood-stained silk scarf monogrammed with the initials C. C.. "The victim had this in her hand when she was found. It makes sense that it belonged to her, but I just wanted you to see it. It looks like it was used to bind a bullet wound on her hand. That's where the blood stains came from."

"Poor Claire." Reginald looked down at the initialed silk scarf and shook his head.

Several hours later Reginald breathed a sigh of relief when he heard the sound of the Ford roadster roaring up the driveway and the squeal of brakes.

Alexis came busting into the front door several moments later, shadowed by Dominic, trying his best to keep the worried, uncle, look from his countenance. Reginald did not want to appear overly concerned either and allowed her to speak first.

"Reggie, you'll never believe where I've been all afternoon."

"Enlighten us please." He had difficulty keeping his harsh tone at bay.

"Oh, I know I should have called you sooner, but I couldn't get to a phone. I was at Bruno's mansion, having a late lunch, with the fat man himself. Can you believe it?"

"Yes, and no. Yes, I believe he would invite you to his house. No, not just for lunch."

"What are you trying to insinuate? Stop looking at me that way Reggie."

"I am not insinuating anything, but why would Von Heller invite you over for lunch?"

"I think Bruno actually likes me; my work I mean. Why don't you settle down and let me finish telling you?"

"I'm listening." He crossed his arms. Dominic leaned against the wall.

"He didn't invite me over. I went to his house on my own after I found out we weren't shooting today and he was not at work. I had to speak with him in private and this gave me the perfect chance."

"The perfect chance to get yourself killed," Reginald stated.

"But Bruno isn't the killer. If you'll just let me finish I'll tell you what I found out."

"All right then. Please continue."

"It turns out Bruno is allergic to tobacco smoke. That's why he left the club in such a hurry last night and why he was in bed all morning and not at work. He tried to smoke a cigar at the club last night. It made him deathly ill."

"Yes, I saw him with a huge cigar," Reginald nodded.

"Well, I managed to get myself past his butler and into his mansion and he actually seemed pleased to see me."

"He probably wanted to eat you for lunch."

Alexis kicked his shin. "Ouch."

"He was sitting up, but still looked a little green when I saw him. He told me about the allergic reaction and invited me to eat some soup and cold sandwiches. They tasted very good. I should try to make some for us sometime," Alexis continued excitedly.

"Alexis. What did he tell you?" Reginald asked impatiently.

"We talked about the picture, and all, and then I asked him about his life and work. He seemed to brighten when he talked about himself, as you can imagine. He started talking about his successful film career and all of his brilliant movies."

"It's difficult to believe he would talk so much about himself," Reginald added sarcastically.

"After he talked about his work for what seemed like an eternity, I asked him about his early life. He told me about his childhood in Germany and everything about his family, and guess what Reggie?"

"What?"

"Bruno Von Heller never had a brother."

"Sure he did, my girl. Max said …." Suddenly he remembered the bloody scarf and his face became ashen.

"Reggie? What is it?" she asked with concern.

"I know who the murderer is Alexis. The one who caused Lillian's death and is responsible for the other killings too."

"Tell me."

He told her about a woman seen falling from the Studio's stolen biplane this morning.

Murder By Plane 185.

"I went down to the police station to find out more information and to try to convince them there was a killer."

"Any luck?"

"They told me the body was Claire Cauldwell."

"Oh, no. What a way for her to die. But how do they know who the killer is?"

"They don't, but I do. Sergeant Atkins showed me a silk scarf found with the body. It had the initials C.C. monogrammed on it."

"What would be so unusual about that Reggie? C.C. for Claire Cauldwell?"

"But it was a silk flying scarf from the war. A man's scarf."

"Then who's initials where they?"

"Clyde Carver."

"Clyde Carver? Are you telling me that it's Max?"

"Max was a nickname he received as a flyer in the war. Maximum Carver. He always wanted to be first at everything and continually pushed his luck. The rest of us just wanted to do our job and survive, but he seemed to actually enjoy killing.

Yes, it is all coming to me now. I remember how I saw him gun down German airmen who were trying to surrender. They had survived a crash and were wounded on the ground. Max dove his plane and machine-gunned both men. I thought he had done it by accident, or so I tried to tell myself at the time. It was during the heat of battle and I was fighting to stay alive too.

I had forgotten about it until just now. Max is a cold blooded killer."

"He made up the story about Bruno having a brother in the war to throw us off track."

"Yes, but I still don't know what his motive is for sabotaging my plane."

"What about Claire? What part did she have in all of this?"

"Claire was insane and she possessed some sort of

delusion that revolved around me, as you found out at the club last night. Undoubtedly, Max was using her to do some of his dirty work for him. When she became too difficult to control and risked drawing attention to him, he disposed of her."

"Terrible. But can we prove any of this Reggie?"

"Not without more evidence. I don't think a silk scarf is enough and the man is a lawyer."

"He can't know we are on to him yet. Maybe we could find more evidence."

"Yes, I'm sure he must be hiding his trophies somewhere."

"Trophies?"

"The man is a sadistic killer. He enjoys it and probably keeps some sort of reminder around."

"That's creepy. Did he do that during the war?"

"Sometimes, when he could, but it was wartime and most men behave rather strangely."

"What are we going to do now?"

"We are going to have dinner."

"What? We can't just take time to eat. We have to find a way to prove Max is the killer."

"All in good time, my girl. As you said earlier, he does not know that we know. We must approach this logically. It would not do for us to go smashing into his office in broad daylight."

"So we wait until dark and break into his office?"

"Now you are beginning to think like me," he said.

"I don't know if that's a compliment or an insult."

Reginald ignored her comment and calmly walked toward the dinning room. "I had Maria prepare something for us before she left this evening. I am famished."

Chapter 19.

It was after ten o'clock when they parked the Ford roadster far enough away to avoid close scrutiny, yet close enough for a quick getaway from Carver's office. A few scattered streetlights cast circles of illumination along the block. The air was still and warm as the two actors exited the roadster and scurried along the sidewalk. They instinctively knew to keep their communication to a minimum. When they had reached the door to the office Reginald used the skeleton key to open it. It appeared the pair was entering a familiar place to anyone walking or driving by.

"You don't suppose Max may still be hanging around do you?" the girl asked.

"That would be highly unlikely. He is, no doubt, at home by now planning our funerals."

"That's a pretty scary thought Reggie. Can we please just hurry up so we can get out of here as quickly as possible?"

"Sorry, my girl, the man really is dangerous and we must approach him with caution, but we must not allow him to know we are on to him." He switched on his flashlight.

"It's a good thing we're actors," she said.

"Yes, but I do not want this to be our last performance either."

"Will you please stop with the morbidlyness?"

"I do not think morbidlyness is a real word." He again used the special key to open the inner office.

"Well, you know what I mean, smarty-pants. You're enjoying this aren't you?"

"Not really, but I do feel as if a weight has been lifted from my shoulders. I can't explain it, or at least not at the moment," he said quietly.

"Maybe we should discuss it all after we're done committing our third felony," she added.

188. T.E.Avery

"I think this may be our fourth felony together. We should start by searching the desk first. If he keeps anything meaningful in his office it would, most likely, be there."

Reginald went to the cluttered desk and began looking around. "Let us start with this top drawer."

"I'll keep watch by the door while you search the desk."

"Good idea. Wait, here is something," he said.

"What is it?"

"This note paper on the desk top. Do you remember the scrap of paper we found at the hanger when Don Denison was killed?"

"You mean the tiny piece of paper with the numbers and drop of blood on it?"

"It was the same type of paper as this. Max probably never knew he dropped the paper at the crime scene," Reginald stated.

"Probably not."

"That was easy, now I'll begin looking inside the drawers and see if I find anything else of interest."

"What if he notices his things have been moved around?" Alexis asked.

"Perhaps it would not be such a bad idea to let him know we are on to him."

"Oh, are you saying we should flush him out?" she asked.

"Why not turn the hunter into the hunted for a change?"

Reginald had searched all the desk drawers except the large one on the bottom left. A lock did not deter him from getting inside it.

"Did you find any other evidence?"

"Here are tools that may have belonged to an aircraft mechanic. Tools that could have been used to loosen bolts on an aircraft undercarriage."

"But how are we going to prove that to the police? We can't call them from this office and ask them to come over. If Max discovers we've been snooping around he'll get rid of the evidence."

"Yes, I see your point. This proves Max was at the hanger and probably tampered with the wheel of the Nieuport, but it is still not enough."

"Should we take the stuff with us or just leave it?"

"I think we should remove the notepaper and tools so Max will realize we are onto him."

"Yeah, let's see what he does when he finds out we've been here."

"I just want to take a quick look around in here one more time before we go. Did you notice something different from the last time we were here?"

"Now that you mention it, I think I did. Wait a minute Reggie. Everything in this office is old except one thing."

"This desk lamp. Max replaced his old lamp because he used it to start the fire at the studio."

"What a creep. He wanted the fire to appear like an accident," she said.

"I think Carver has put great effort in making almost everything look like an accident."

"What do you think he will do when he discovers we've been here?" she asked, as Reginald closed the door on their way out.

"My hope is that he will panic and begin to make mistakes. Eventually we will have something we can use to trap him," Reginald said.

After they walked back to the car, glancing around to make sure no one had been watching them; Alexis asked the very question that had been on his mind.

"But what if he doesn't panic Reggie? What if he just keeps killing people?"

After returning to Reginald's house, they seemed to be naturally drawn into the comfortable study where he poured them both a small glass of his best whisky.

190. T.E.Avery

"Thanks, I think I need this to help me relax after this day," she said.

"Yes, it has been an extremely tense day for both of us. At least we now know who the murderer is."

"I still can't believe someone could pose as your best friend for years, but be a fiend, capable of murder."

"I know, it is difficult to imagine, but most people are not what they seem."

"But to be such a cold blooded killer? Do you think his mind snapped during the war?"

"No, I think he must have been born without a soul, even drawn to the war, in order to kill for pleasure."

"How are we going to unmask this monster without getting ourselves or others killed?"

"We must have patience and go about our business as usual until he slips up and we have something that can be brought to the authorities," Reginald said.

"How soon do you think it will be before he discovers we were in his office?"

"I deliberately left several drawers slightly open so he should be immediately aware his office was broken into."

"But how will Max know that it was us snooping around?"

"With no sign of forced entry and nothing removed except mementoes of the crimes he committed? I think he will know it was us, or at least me."

"Do you have any idea what his actions may be after he finds out that we know it's him?"

"My guess would be that he will attempt to find and eliminate the one witness who can place him at the scene of the crime."

"Joe Fisk. But Fisk is in the desert, isn't he?" Alexis asked.

"But Max now has the Nieuport biplane. He must have a small grass strip he is using as a runway. Perhaps it is one of those old fields we used back in the silent movie days. If he discovers we are on to him he may go to the plane and use it to get to Barstow as quickly as possible. From there he could search for Fisk, find him, and kill the old man before anyone else finds him. He may even know where Fisk is staying and has been in no hurry to eliminate him. Of course that will all change tomorrow when he discovers we know he is the killer."

"With Fisk out of the picture we wouldn't have a chance proving that he did it. What can we do?" she asked.

"We will need to follow Max when he leaves his office tomorrow. We can stay out of sight in the roadster. He can't outrun us."

"Maybe we should get the police involved Reggie. If they find him with the stolen biplane he may confess to the other crimes as well."

"What do we tell the police? That we think a lawyer has stolen a Nieuport biplane from the Studio and we need them to follow him? They do not take kindly to being instructed in criminal investigations by civilians."

"I see what you mean. So it's up to us to close in on this psychotic killer and find a way to stop him before he gets into the plane."

"You have to be at work in the morning. I will take Dominic with me in the Ford for backup."

"No. I'm going too. I don't care about the movie. Besides, Bruno has put the film off for another day while he recuperates."

"Alexis, we are dealing with a crazed murderer. I cannot allow you to be put in harms way. I must insist this time. Dominic and I will follow Max and stop him before he boards the biplane."

"But I've been in this from the start Reggie. I came here to find my sister's murderer and I want to bring him to justice." Her eyes were brimming with tears now.

"You did find the killer, my girl, and you will see him brought to justice, but if I allow you to accompany us and something happens to you, I could never forgive myself."

Now she was getting angry. "So it's all about you and your feelings? Well, what about me Reggie? I want to be there when we catch the creep who killed my sister. I want to see the look on his face when he finally gets caught."

"Sorry Alexis, but you can't come with me this time. You can wait here by the telephone and have the honor of calling the police after we stop Max."

Her eyes flashed fire, but she maintained her control, as an idea began to form in the back of her mind. "All right then, if that's the way it has to be." She wiped her eyes with the back of her hand.

"Good. I'm glad you finally see it is for your best interest," Reginald said with relief.

"Yeah, I suppose you're right."

"You'll stay here tonight of course. I will tell Dominic our plans while you ready yourself for bed." He finished his drink and stood.

It was after midnight when Reginald finally decided to leave his study and go upstairs to bed. He was troubled by thoughts of tomorrow's plans and the possible disasters that could occur when dealing with someone as unpredictable as Max Carver. His mind was racing when he looked up. Alexis was standing in the doorway dressed in her nightgown and a flimsy see-through robe.

Images of Lillian flashed through his mind as he was reminded of that day, a few short weeks ago, when he had mistaken the girl for the specter of her dead sister.

"Oh, I thought you would be asleep by this time, my girl," he said.

She came into the room and sat on the arm of his chair. She placed her hand on his neck and her fingers lightly touched his hair.

"I can't sleep. I keep thinking about Lillian and how she died so suddenly, so young and needlessly. It just doesn't make sense. Why did he have to take her life?"

"No one can answer that question except the killer

himself. He could not have known she would be in my plane that day. It had to be me he was after. For some reason Max wanted me to have an accident that day."

"But why? It all just seems so senseless."

"Yes, he caused the death of a person who meant so much to so many people."

"What kind of love did you and Lillian share Reggie?"

"We loved each other; were in love. What else is there?"

"Was it an all consuming love? Was it the special kind of love that two people have when you walk into a room full of people, but all you see is each other? Did you love everything about each other?"

Reginald thought about it for several minutes before answering. "No. To be honest, I really don't think it was that kind of love, now that you mention it."

"Have you ever experienced the sort of love I'm talking about?" she asked.

"No, have you?" The meager lighting darkened half of her face when he tried to look into her eyes.

"No, but I would like to know that kind of love one day," she said.

"Do you really believe two people can love that way?" Reginald asked.

"Yes. I do," she whispered.

Chapter 20.

Reginald and Dominic wanted to find a good place from which to observe Carver's office so they left very early the next morning. Alexis was up before the two men and managed to prepare them a small breakfast. She also wrapped some of Maria's tasty enchiladas and put them in a paper bag with a thermos of fresh coffee. At least they wouldn't go hungry while staking out the killer's workplace.

Alexis felt guilty for assuring Reginald that she would wait by the phone for his call to let her know when Max was apprehended. She hated to lie to Reginald, but there was no way she could allow them to go after the murderer without her. She justified her actions by telling herself she had every right to follow the two men. The hard part would be staying out of sight in the big Duesenberg.

She found the keys, on a hook, in Dominic's garage apartment. Alexis thought about the danger she could be in as she turned the key and the engine thundered to life and settled into a throaty rumble. She pulled the Duesenberg out of the garage, closed the double doors and roared away.

"We been watchin this place for a long time now boss. You think anybody in there?"

"It has been precisely one hour and nineteen minutes Dominic. That is not very long in a stakeout and I am sure our friend will make his move soon enough."

"He not my friend boss. I never like that guy too much anyway." The big man shook his head and frowned.

"One never knows what is in the deep recesses of a man's heart Dominic."

Dominic had parked the roadster across the street and partially hidden behind a corner of a brick building.

Murder By Plane 195.

Little did they know Alexis, in the Duesenberg, was parked half a block behind them in an alley between two office buildings.

"Look boss, the man. He comin out now."

"Good. Now if he will just go where I think he will. Perfect. He is pulling away now. Let's get after him Dominic."

Dominic pulled the Ford out into the stream of traffic and began following Carver's large black Packard.

"He going pretty fast boss."

"Try to stay back far enough that he doesn't observe us Dominic."

"I try boss."

"Don't let him get out of sight."

Dominic struggled to navigate through busy streets, while keeping the other car in sight without overtaking it.

"Don't worry. I'm doing the best I can do boss."

"I know Dominic, I'm just getting a little excited. I promise I will allow you to do the driving from this point on; old friend."

Alexis knew she had to stay out of sight while also keeping up with the Ford. This was no easy task with a car that stood out in traffic like a beauty queen in a room full of old ladies. Her plan was to stay behind them until Carver was somehow subdued by Reginald and Dominic. Once the killer was captured, she would drive up to the scene with a smile on her face.

She thought about all they had gone through to get to this point. She had been sure Von Heller was the murderer. He'd had the motive, the opportunity and the method, or so it had seemed to her. And what about poor Claire? What had her role been in all of this? Her thoughts turned back to Reginald and Dominic in the car ahead of her. She wondered how they would handle the situation when they finally confronted Carver.

She could see in the distance they were getting to the edge of town. It was getting increasingly more difficult to keep up with the roadster. She knew she was taking a chance when she decided to follow her heart; making plans without consulting Reginald.

"He's going to kill me when he finds out," she said aloud.

Now the Ford was only a tiny dot on the horizon and Alexis considered her options if she completely lost sight of them. She could head back to the beach house, although she didn't really want to. What if she became lost and Reginald tried to phone her?

"No, I won't get lost," she said with resolve.

She could see the general direction that they had taken and there were few side streets. This had to be the road they were on and it was taking them away from the city. This was becoming more of a farm road with hard pavement, turning into gravel, as she continued along.

The gravel threw up clouds of dust behind the big car as Alexis pressed her foot to the accelerator. She hoped a farm tractor or a team of mules didn't suddenly appear as she rounded a bend in the grimy road. As the Duesenberg followed the curve of a large hill, Alexis nearly panicked at the scene that filled the windshield before her.

The Ford was on its side in the middle of the road and Reginald was kneeling beside Dominic's prone form nearby. He looked up just as she slammed on the brakes to keep from running them over. Reginald's eyes locked on Alexis's. She jumped out of the Duesenberg before it stopped rolling and ran to Reginald's side.

"Reggie, what's happened?"

"Max was waiting for us when we rounded the hill. He came out of that side road and slammed into us. Dominic got the worst of it."

She looked down at Dominic and could see the big Italian was unconscious, but still breathing.

"Is he going to be okay?" she asked with concern.

"I think so, but we must get him to a hospital soon. It looks as if he may have a broken arm and perhaps a concussion."

"We can't carry him. What will we do?"

"You turn the Duesenberg around and I will see if I can get him awake. It is not good to allow someone with a concussion to remain unconscious."

Alexis did as she was told. Dominic, having regained consciousness, and with Reginald's help, was able to limp a few feet to the car. The big man all but collapsed into the back seat and Reginald climbed in with him to administer battlefield first aid.

"Do you think he will be all right?" she glanced into the rearview mirror after starting the car.

"I don't know what other injuries he may have, but it looks like he will make it if we can get him to a doctor."

"I'm so glad I followed my instincts and didn't stay home." She put the car into gear and threw gravel in her haste to get Dominic to the care that could save his life.

"Yes, how did you manage to find us out here?"

She sheepishly told Reginald how she left the beach house and had parked just down the street from their stakeout, following them through town until she lost sight of them.

"I'm sorry Reggie, but I just had this strong urge to follow along. I wanted to be here with you and Dominic."

"I know I should be upset about it, especially with your subterfuge, but it is a good thing that you followed your instincts," he agreed.

"Thanks for not getting angry with me."

"As a pilot I know how important it can be to rely on instinct."

They managed to arrive at the hospital without incident and the emergency personnel carried Dominic into the triage area. Reginald and Alexis followed close behind.

"I hope he's going to be okay."

198. T.E.Avery

"He is a fighter and I think he will pull through just fine. I do feel rather badly about the whole thing though. It was my plan and now it has caused Dominic to be injured and Max has gotten away."

"Dominic knew it was going to be dangerous Reggie, but he went with you anyway. He wanted to catch Max as much as you did."

"I suppose you are right," Reginald said.

"So what now? Are we back to square one?"

"I don't know. Let's get Dominic settled in and make sure he will be all right and then I may have a plan B."

"I sure hope, for our sakes, that it works better than your plan A."

"Thank you for your vote of confidence ... Kansas," he answered dryly.

"Do you think you can find the airfield Reggie?"

"I hope I remember where it is. It has been many years since I have gone there. I only hope that my hunch is correct." Reginald was behind the wheel of the Duesenberg this time and driving at a rapid pace.

"If Carver is still there he is most likely armed and dangerous. Maybe we should have called the police," Alexis said.

"What could we tell them to make them follow us out into the country after a lunatic lawyer?"

"I guess you're right, but I hope just the two of us will be enough to stop him."

"You will wait in the relative safety of the car while I investigate the scene. If ... something happens to me, you must drive away as fast as possible and call the police."

"Reggie I ...."

"No arguments this time, my girl. It is the most practical approach. I will be armed with my revolver and you will be my rear guard. Do you have your own pistol?"

"It's still in my purse. I suppose you're right, somebody has to guard your rear," she smiled.

"Touché. Now if I can just remember where that blasted airfield is. It was only a small grass strip on a farm with an old house and a barn. We used it to practice our stunt routines back in the silent film days. Some of the aerial action scenes were shot there for various pictures."

After topping a hill, they spotted what seemed to be a small airplane, half hidden, behind an old barn about a hundred yards across a plowed field. "Oh look Reggie, could that be the farm?"

"Yes, that is the place," he downshifted and decreased their speed as they came closer.

They could see the black Packard, its front bumper bent, parked hastily beside the barn. The large barn door was open, swinging slightly in the breeze like a beckoning hand. Reginald parked the Duesenberg along the rutted dirt driveway. Without being sure where the madman was hiding, he did not want to provide an easy target.

"Stay here and watch for any movement from the barn or house. Keep your pistol ready and don't be afraid to use it. Just be careful who you shoot," he cautioned.

"What are you going to do?" she asked.

"I am going to circle around and through the back of the barn. If it proves to be empty I will go into the house."

"Please be careful Reggie."

"I promise that I will. I am not anxious to be shot." She suddenly placed her hands on each side of his face, pulled him close and kissed him full on the mouth. "For luck."

"Thank you. Please stay in the car and do as we discussed earlier."

He ran along the plowed field that bordered the property and around the back of the dilapidated barn. He

200. T.E.Avery

carefully looked through the decrepit structure with his pistol pointed in front of him. After several tense minutes, Reginald felt satisfied Max Carver was not hiding within and he walked out through the large front doors. A quick glance in the Duesenberg's direction confirmed that Alexis was all right. He carefully approached the small house. Stepping onto the back porch, he slowly opened the door and peered into the gloom of a dusty back room. The door hinges squeaked as he pushed the wooden panel with one hand and kept the gun trained on the area before him.

Alexis decided to follow Reginald's instructions this time and stayed near the car. She didn't know why she kissed him before he left, but she had not regretted her spontaneous action. The man was risking his life after all, she reasoned, smiling to herself when she thought about the look on his face. He had been completely surprised and so had she.

She leaned against the car, unconcerned about the dust, watching for any sign that someone could be hiding in the buildings. Alexis decided that if she saw anything suspicious she would try to warn Reginald in some way. She had not determined what she would do to sound the alarm. Maybe call out or scream, she thought, or perhaps fire the small pistol that was now clutched in her hand.

Alexis began to experience a feeling of dread until Reginald appeared at the front of the barn, glancing her way. Not knowing what to do, she raised her arm in a small wave. He trotted toward the house, disappearing inside. It seemed like a very long time before he finally emerged, but it had only been about ten minutes. She breathed a sigh of relief at the sight of him. He walked quickly back to the car.

"It looks like no one is home," he said.

"Are you sure he's not in there? Maybe he's hiding behind something."

"No, if that were the case I am sure he would have done something by now."

"But that's his car over there, isn't it?" she asked.

"Yes, I'm sure that is the car that rammed us. I found some tire tracks that looked like they belonged to the Nieuport."

"So you think he took off from here?"

"Yes, he has been using this strip as a kind of headquarters. It even appears that Claire may have been living in the house. I found some things, belonging to a woman, while I was searching the place."

"What a dreadful existence she must have had. What is that other plane over near the barn Reggie?"

"That is a Monocoupe 70. Max must have kept it out here too. Perhaps he used it for business purposes."

"Where do you think he went?"

"In search of Joe Fisk, where else? Mr. Fisk is the only one who can positively place Max at the hanger on the night before the sabotage. Max had no good reason to be there and in fact, was an intruder."

"So he's flying out, to wherever Joe Fisk is, to kill him?"

"That would be my guess," Reginald said.

Chapter 21.

"Reggie, we have to stop him. We can't let him murder the only witness we have."

"What do you propose we should do? Max is probably halfway to Barstow by now. It would take us hours to navigate back across the city and then wind our way through the mountains."

Crows cawed in the trees nearby as the two actors stared at each other in silence.

"I know. We can take the other airplane," Alexis said excitedly.

"I don't know if that is a very sound idea Alexis," Reginald said.

"Why not? You can fly. I bet you know how to fly almost any airplane ever made."

"Well, I ah ... I do not even know if that airplane has any fuel in its tank."

"You could check it couldn't you? I bet you could look at that plane and tell if it's flyable, couldn't ya?"

"Alexis, I must be honest with you. I have not felt a desire to fly in a long time."

"You mean since the accident?"

"Yes, in fact, the thought of getting in a cockpit again makes my stomach churn."

"Are you telling me that you are scared?"

"Well, yes. I suppose so. If you want to know the truth, I am terrified."

"Oh great. So what are we supposed to do now? Give up?"

"We could call the police."

"But you, yourself, have said, repeatedly, they won't help us unless we get more proof. Are we going to just stand here and let that evil man, who murdered my sister, get away?"

"I suppose I could have a look at the Monocoupe, but it may not be in working order." She followed his steps across the farmyard toward the small two-seat plane.

The Monocoupe 70 was the first private, two-seat,

aircraft available to the general public. It had an enclosed cockpit with side by side seating. The company was started in the twenties and produced the first Monocoupe in 1927. Reginald began inspecting the small plane by checking the fuel and oil.

"There is plenty of gas in the tank. I will walk around and inspect the wings and fuselage." He took hold of a wing strut and shook it vigorously.

"Why are you doing that?" Alexis asked.

"I want to make sure the wings will stay on."

"Oh, yeah ... good idea," she giggled nervously.

Reginald continued to carefully examine the aircraft.

"It looks to be in good shape. Let's turn her around facing the strip."

The two moved the light airplane so that it was lined up with the grass airstrip and facing into the wind. Reginald looked up at the sky. He seemed to be deep in thought.

"Reggie, are you okay?"

"What? Oh, yes ... I ... I am fine. Perhaps you should stay here with the car while I fly over to Barstow."

"Oh no. I'm not staying behind. What if that nut comes back here? Besides, I want to find him too."

"Well, if you insist, but anything could happen. At least the weather is in our favor."

"Oh boy. I've never flown before." He could see a mixture of excitement and fear in her face that reminded him of her sister.

"Are you sure you will be all right?" he asked.

"Yes, now let's go before Carver gets too far away."

Reginald instructed her how to turn the switch after he had primed the engine. He stood at the front of the plane and rotated the propeller around by hand. He turned the wooden prop several times, slowly, and then he gave it a powerful downward push. The first try was unsuccessful, but after several more attempts, the engine shuttered to life with a puff of smoke from the exhaust.

Reginald went around to the pilot's seat.

"I'm glad it finally started," she yelled above the noisy motor.

"Here we go. Are you properly strapped in?"

"I think so," she said from the seat beside him.

Reginald taxied the Monocoupe to the field and lined it up in the middle of the runway without stopping. He pushed the throttle in all the way to the consol and the little plane rolled faster along the grass. The tail of the plane came up after a few seconds and he allowed the speed to build before he slowly pulled back on the stick. The wheels lifted off the grass and they were in the air. They barely cleared a clump of bushes at the end of the runway and now it seemed they were headed straight for the side of a hill. After what seemed the last moment, Reginald pointed the nose a little higher and they flew over the top of the ridge.

Alexis looked over at his face, and saw no sign of fear. She watched as he nimbly moved the controls and realized he was in his own element. After Reginald climbed to three thousand feet and leveled off, he throttled back and the engine settled into a steady drone.

She began to relax and enjoy the scenery below them.

"Oh look. The buildings are so small and the cars look like toys."

"We will head east and go over the mountains. There should be a map in here somewhere."

"Here's one. Do you want me to look for something on the map?"

"I just want to get my bearings and sense of direction. I pretty much know which way we need to go. We can follow the terrain below."

"If you say so. It all looks so different from way up here." She suddenly began to feel some anxiety.

"You just relax and we will be over the mountains before you know it," he said calmly.

"Okay, I'm relaxing now. I just felt a moment of panic."

Murder By Plane 205.

"That is understandable with this being your first flight. How do you like it so far?"

"It feels strangely exciting, but peaceful. It's like nothing I've ever experienced before."

"Well, I'm glad you are not terrified. It would not do to have a frightened female aboard," he said.

"Well, this was my idea. Hey, what was that funny noise?"

Before she could even turn her head to ask him again, Reginald had turned the plane so sharply on its side that all she could see was blue sky. She felt the blood rushing out of her head as a gray blur flashed by to her right.

"What are you doing?" she screamed.

"We have company." He gripped the controls while swinging his head around for a better look through the windshield. Alexis followed his gaze and could see that the blur she had briefly experienced was the Nieuport biplane. It was above them now and climbing steeply.

"What is he doing Reggie?"

"That is an Immelmann turn," he said. "He is going to half loop and dive down again."

"What are you going to do?" she asked fearfully.

"The only thing that I can do, my girl."

He rolled the little Monocoupe and dove downward as steeply as possible.

"Oh no. Reggie." she screamed.

"Hold on. We must get down on the deck. The Nieuport has one flaw."

"What?"

"The canvas on the upper wings can rip off in a power dive."

"What about this plane?"

"I don't know. I have never flown a Monocoupe before."

"What? Are we going to die?"

"Not if I can help it," Reginald shouted above the engines whine.

206. T.E.Avery

Reginald pulled out of the dive just before reaching tree top level. He turned his head around to see what had become of Carver.

"He could not have descended as fast as we did, but he will be on us soon."

He kept the Monocoupe level now and pushed the throttle in as far as it would go. The little plane shot forward to its maximum speed.

"I wonder what he plans to do next Reggie?"

"It just depends," he said.

"Depends? Depends on what?"

The Monocoupe shook violently as bullets pierced the canvas and shattered the windshield.

"Keep your head down Alexis. He is using live ammunition in those guns. I was afraid of that."

"We're going to die. We're going to die. Oh God." Alexis buried her head in her lap.

"Don't give up yet, my girl. We have one thing in our favor."

"What?" She yelled as another round of bullets slammed into the plane.

"I was always a better pilot than Max." He turned the plane tightly to port. The blood rushed from their heads.

Carver turned with them, struggling to stay on the Monocoupe's tail. Reginald turned again and headed for the Hollywood hills. They could see the Hollywoodland sign on the mountainside far away; the hills, houses and streets sprawling below. The sign looked small, but grew larger every second. Both planes flew at more than one hundred twenty miles per hour. Reginald kept turning right and left. He knew Carver, with his bad leg, would have trouble pushing the rudder pedal. All the while a plan formed in his mind as he fought to keep them from their final act.

When the Hollywoodland sign had grown large enough to fill the area where the windshield had been, Reginald waited until Carver was closing in for the kill.

Murder By Plane 207.

At the last second he abruptly pulled up and turned the plane over on its side, skidding sideways in the air. It was a bold and dangerous move, but it allowed them to slow down dramatically as the Nieuport shot past under them. Carver slammed into the sign, between the two L's, at maximum speed.

The biplane did not explode on impact, but crumpled like a piece of cardboard as the wings folded backward and broke off. Reginald and Alexis heard the crash as he struggled with the controls of the little Monocoupe. He managed to sweep along the side of the hill, feet away from trees, and lightly brought the aircraft down onto a nearby road, barely missing a telephone line and several parked automobiles. People ran away while some were stepping out of their cars and houses for a better look.

Reginald sat still for several seconds, took a deep breath and turned to Alexis. Her head remained face down in her lap and she wasn't moving.

"Alexis? Are you all right?"

"Is it over?" She slowly raised her head.

"Yes, it's over." He looked up at the smoldering wreck on the hillside. "The murder biplane is gone forever."

Epilogue

By the time Reginald and Alexis managed to hitch a ride to the road leading up to the sign, hiking the last half mile on foot, they could see several police and other emergency personnel had already arrived.

The biplane had crashed into the huge symbol of the film industry that stood just below the mountain's summit, causing the entire structure to lean backward. Most of the sign remained intact, but the airplane had gone between the two "L's" with devastating results. The Nieuport's wings were sheared off and the fuselage smoldered in a heap on the hillside.

"Did the pilot survive?" Reginald asked a policeman as he and Alexis approached.

"Yeah, but I don't know how long he'll last cause he's in bad shape. He must have been a lunatic to fly that plane into the sign. We were trying to identify the guy. What are you two doing up here anyhow?" The cop removed his cap to rub a hand across a thinning hairline.

"We know who he is," Alexis said.

"Well, they got him over there on a blanket. I guess you can go over, but I'm warning you, it might be tough to look at."

"Perhaps you should remain here Alexis," Reginald said.

"No. I need to see him. I can take it after all we've been through."

She immediately regretted her words after they approached the crumpled form covered by a red blanket. Half of Carver's face remained the only recognizable feature. Most of the right side and top of his head were covered in bloody bandages. An attendant knelt at his side. The medic glanced up as Reginald walked over.

"How is he Doctor?"

"I'm not a doctor, I'm just an ambulance attendant, but I can tell you, he's in bad shape."

"Is he conscious?" Reginald asked. Alexis followed close behind.

"He has been mumbling a few words now and then."

Murder By Plane 209.

The medic stood and talked quietly now. "He's busted up real bad inside. I don't think he has much longer. Are you a friend of his?" The man looked down the steep hillside at the plane wreck.

"I knew him, or I thought I did," Reginald stated. He knelt close to the dying Max.

"Max, can you hear me?" Reginald asked.

"I hear you Reg," Max Carver said weakly after a long moment. His one uncovered eye opened slightly, but he could not move his head.

"Why Max?"

"You... you had to be so good. You even got... Lillian." The words came out slowly, but full of venom. His one eye glared fiercely, but then faded into lifelessness.

"Is he dead?" Alexis gulped.

"Yes, Max is gone."

They were both startled as the fiery biplane exploded. The flames had finally reached the fuel tank and the rescue workers did not have access to water to put the fire out. Everyone stood and watched the, once beautiful, airplane burning on the hillside below.

Two weeks later Reginald and Alexis sat at the patio table, enjoying the first cool breeze they had felt in a long time. Alexis prepared breakfast for them that morning and the two discussed different subjects, including her career and future, before the topic turned to the events of the last few weeks.

"So Carver secretly hated you all these years because of envy?" she asked. "He sabotaged the biplane to hurt you. Maybe never even intending to cause Lillian's death."

"Yes, I believe that is a correct assumption, Reginald said. Max became obsessed with out-performing me during the war. He ruthlessly killed unarmed enemy pilots, men who had already surrendered, in order to claim victories. But Max was never a great pilot and finally crashed his plane in a stunt accident after the war. This probably led to him becoming even angrier."

"Crazed, if you ask me, Alexis said. "Do you think he became fixated with Lillian too? Maybe she was the one thing he and Claire shared in common. Claire became infatuated with you and he with Lillian."

"Yes, perhaps. And maybe that is why Max set the fire at the studio. Von Heller's people had gathered incriminating evidence that proved Max wanted Lillian for himself."

"Yeah, he tried to make it look like an accident too, by using that old lamp from his office to set the fire," she added.

"He tried to make the police believe everything was accidental from the start; my plane crash, the fire and Brogan and Denison's deaths. It all started again when I called him about hiring a private detective. He probably thought Brogan, the bumbling slacker, would fail to turn anything up, but Brogan got lucky and found out about Joe Fisk. I'm sure Max would have made Joe Fisk come to an end in some clever way too."

"If only Carver could have known that the old codger had died of heat stroke in the desert," she added.

"He set Claire up as a disguised, replacement, cook to keep tabs on me after he injured poor Grace in her car wreck."

"He ended up putting half of your staff out of commission Reggie. I'm glad Dominic is back on his feet. I don't know why he refused to eat breakfast with us."

"Sicilian pride I suppose," Reginald laughed.

"When will Grace be back to work?" she asked.

"In a few more weeks," Reginald said.

"You mentioned something a few days ago about a letter from Claire."

"Yes. The police found it with her things at the

Murder By Plane 211.

abandoned farmhouse Carver had her living in; the place with the small airstrip. She had wanted to warn me about Carver, but obviously never got the chance."

"Do you think that's why he killed her?" she asked.

"Probably. It could also be that she was becoming more difficult to control and he wanted her out of the way. He used the biplane to dispose of her too."

"That's so sad. I hate that I wounded her," Alexis said.

"You had no other choice at the time, my girl. What are your plans now?"

"I need to go back home to settle my father's estate.

After that I may come back here to try and get acting work, unless Von Heller has blackballed me all over town."

"I doubt it. I think the evil, fat, spider may actually like you."

"A scary thought, even if he didn't cause my sister's death."

"I still feel somewhat responsible for her dying," he said.

"But you couldn't have known the plane had been sabotaged Reggie."

"Oh, I know. I'm sure I will be able to move on now, even though I'll always harbor some sadness when I think of her." He looked into the girl's green eyes. So lovely, he thought.

"I'll always feel sad too Reggie, but I'll never blame you." She took his hand, leaned forward and pressed her lips tightly against his.

CPSIA information can be obtained at www.ICGtesting.com
Printed in the USA
LVOW070052121012

302561LV00007B/25/P